W9-BFR-257

Union Army Black

L. Travis teaches English at a Minnesota college and lectures frequently on fantasy and literature.

Ben and Zack Series, Book 4

Union Army Black

L. Travis

Baker Books

A Division of Baker Book House Co
Grand Rapids, Michigan 49516

© 1995 by L. Travis

Published by Baker Books
a division of Baker Book House Company
P.O. Box 6287, Grand Rapids, Michigan 49516–6287

Printed in the United States of America

All rights reserved. No part of this publication may be reproduced, stored in a retrieval system, or transmitted in any form or by any means—for example, electronic, photocopy, recording—without the prior written permission of the publisher. The only exception is brief quotations in printed reviews.

Library of Congress Cataloging-in-Publication Data

Travis, Lucille, 1931–
    Union army black / L. Travis.
      p. cm. — (Ben and Zack series; bk. 4)
    Summary: A twelve-year-old black boy who has watched the Civil War continue for four bloody years, enlists as a drummer boy in the Union Army and finds adventure in the Shenandoah Valley of Virginia.
    ISBN 0-8010-4037-X
    1. United States—History—Civil War, 1861–1865—Juvenile fiction. [1. United States—History—Civil War, 1861–1865—Fiction. 2. Afro-Americans—Fiction.] I. Title. II. Series: Travis, L. 1931– Ben and Zack series; bk. 4
PZ.T68915Un 1995
[Fic]—dc20

95-10349

For our own dear
Zach
whose name means
God remembers

Contents

Contents

1

The Runaway

A bitter wind blew down the street, and Zack shoved his hands deeper into his pockets. Only a few weeks into January the winter of 1864 had already brought record cold to New York City. The snow crunched underfoot, but Zack barely noticed. In a few minutes he would catch an omnibus downtown to the army recruitment office, and he would not be coming back. If they would take him, he was determined to join the Union army of the North as a drummer boy. A sharp gust of wind blew his muffler like a red streak across his dark-brown face as he turned for a last sight of his friend. He pulled the muffler down and waved to Ben. A lump rose in his throat. "I'll write," he shouted.

Ben stood coatless in the open doorway of his aunt's house, his white face a blur, his brown hair blown back by the wind. He waved. Zack knew Ben wanted to join up too. But Ben couldn't go against his minister father, who had forbidden him.

In the attic window above Ben, Zack saw a flash of red hair. Ben's cousin Abigail, with her red hair falling in waves about her face, waved. He would miss her. "Goodbye, Miss Fire and Grit," he whispered. "I won't forget you."

As though she had heard him Abigail whispered, "I'll never forget you, Zack." Her soft blue eyes misted with tears. She had overheard Zack tell Ben he wanted to join the army. She knew she could call out to her mother or Ben's to stop him from going, but she wouldn't. He was no one's slave. He had to be free to go, and with all her heart she wished him well. The wind blew his hat backward, and she laughed as his thick bush of black hair ballooned wildly about his head. His dark face stood out against the white snow. She would miss his gentle, kind way of pointing out her own headstrongness, and his good humor. Her rashness was always getting her into trouble. Miss Fire and Grit, he called her, and only Zack could get away with that.

Zack pulled his hat back about his ears, waved once more, and turned away. It was hard to leave. At the sound of a shout and running feet Zack turned around.

Ben raced toward him with a sack in his hands. "You forgot the biscuits I saved for you," Ben said breathing hard. "I'll write you soon as I know where you are." He shivered in the cold as he held out the sack.

"Thanks," Zack said. "These biscuits will do me fine."

"Don't forget," Ben said, "if the army won't take you in, you come on back here."

Zack nodded. "I reckon the army will take me." With the number of war dead and wounded growing as the war between the North and the South over slavery dragged on into its fourth year, the army needed volunteers. Since New Years Day, the anniversary of President Lincoln's freeing the slaves, Zack had known he wanted to go. The fiery speeches calling for volunteers to help save the Union and bring the war to an end had stirred something inside him. He wanted to be part of it all. "Some of them drummer boys ain't much older than you and me," he had said to Ben. "Anyway, guess I'm big for twelve years."

Ben nodded. Zack was right. He knew of at least one twelve-year-old drummer boy in the Union army, and Zack seemed even taller than his twelve years.

"I best be goin' before your ma or your aunt finds out I'm leavin'," Zack said. "You know they won't be pleased about my wantin' to join the army."

"I know," Ben admitted. Ben's family had brought Zack with them to New York City on this visit to his aunt's house. They had been called abolitionists more than once for treating the orphaned Zack like kin. In another week Zack's visit would be over and Ben's father would have sent him back to Tarrytown, New York. Only, Zack didn't want to go back. "Guess you better be off then."

Zack could feel the pain in Ben's voice. "I got to go, Ben. Your pa's been good to me, but now that your pa is plannin' for all of you to live here with your aunt and uncle I got no good reason to go back to Tarrytown. Granny's gone, and Uncle Uriah barely has room enough for himself. I know Mistress Capp wants me to work for her, but I don't want to go back. If the army will have me, that's where I'm goin'."

Ben grasped his friend's hand and shook it. "You know I'd come with you if I could." His teeth were starting to chatter, and his hand felt icy in Zack's.

"You gonna freeze out here," Zack warned. "You better go on in." Ben hugged his shivering body with his arms, then turned and ran to the house without looking back.

Zack thrust the biscuits inside his coat and walked away quickly. At the corner he caught the horse-drawn omnibus, paid the ten-cent fare, and sat down. Somewhere downtown was the Bureau for Colored Troops where he could sign up to join the Union army. The omnibus felt warm after the cold outside. Zack leaned his head against the back of the wooden seat. Across the aisle a matronly white woman bundled in furs stared at him. Zack turned away from her eyes and looked out of the window.

For the first time in his life he was on his own. Some folks might call him a runaway, though he didn't really belong to anyone. He had left without telling Ben's folks, but he was counting on Ben's preacher father to understand once Ben explained. He shifted uncomfortably in his seat as the woman, who continued to stare at him, whispered to the gentleman next to her. Both of them were staring. Zack decided to get off at the nearest stop and walk.

Now that he didn't have a home he supposed he might be a vagrant, a kind of tramp. New York City had a law against vagrant children. Anyone found wandering homeless on the streets could be arrested. The sooner he got to the army station the better.

As the horses pulled the bus away he wished he were still on it. He had forgotten about the cold. He walked quickly till he came to a cross street where a number of stores displayed their wares in bright frosted shop windows. The woman behind the counter of the first, a small bakery, had never heard of the Bureau for Colored Troops. In another a busy clerk waved him out of the store before Zack could finish his sentence. A passing wagon driver, hunched over his horses' reins, shook his head as Zack called out to ask directions.

For an hour Zack searched the city streets. Not many people were out in the cold, but on a street full of small businesses he saw a gentleman and hurried toward him. The man held onto his tall hat with one gloved hand. In the other he carried a stout cane with a brass head.

"Excuse me, sir," Zack said, "I. . . ."

Before Zack could finish, the man raised his cane in a threatening manner. "Be off," he shouted. "We'll have no beggars here. Off, I say, or I'll call the police." The man's dark eyes glittered angrily.

Zack flung his hands up to protect himself from the man's cane, and then he ran. Behind him he heard the man calling, "Stop thief!" The man must have thought he was going to rob him! As if he were indeed a thief, Zack ran and didn't stop until he turned the corner and headed down another street. Breathing hard, he slowed down. The man was not following him, and Zack rested his back against the wall of a building. A few people, poorly dressed for the winter weather, hurried past, but they paid no attention to Zack. "O Lord," he whispered, "please help me." He glanced up the street, and his heart sank.

Not two blocks away a policeman with his night stick swinging at his side was headed Zack's way. The city police were quick to haul away homeless children to the city's shelters and poor houses. Zack walked as quickly as he could to get away without running. He tried not to glance back. Behind him he heard a shout, "You, there, hold on." It had to be the policeman!

With a burst of speed Zack ran up the first side street he came to, then another and another until he was sure he had lost the policeman. The buildings around him were small and old, mostly shops and saloons. In the doorway near him a drunk sat huddled over. Zack had no idea where he was. Ahead of him the buildings looked more and more like the slum tenements he had seen in the city's Five Points neighborhood. He had to find the way out and soon.

Three doors down he came to an alley between two buildings and hurried into it. The alley was dark and slippery underfoot with frozen garbage. Zack ran toward the opening ahead. He didn't see the young black soldier as he emerged from the alley until they collided with a thud.

2

No Escape

Strong hands gripped his shoulders and held him fast. "Just where are you goin', son?" The voice, though it sounded as surprised as Zack felt, held a note of laughter.

Zack looked up quickly. "Sorry, sir. Guess I sure didn't see you." Something in the soldier's dark face looked familiar to Zack. Suddenly Zack remembered. "Weren't you at Cooper Union Hall on New Years Day at the meeting? I heard you talkin' afterward with Chaplain Turner about joining the army," Zack said. "Looks like you signed up."

"Sure did," the young man said. "Can't say I remember your face, but any friend of Chaplain Turner is a friend of mine." He extended his hand to Zack. "Moses Comstead," he said.

Zack shook his hand. "Zack Boone. Chaplain Turner sure is a fine speaker. Made me want to join up right then. I been lookin' for the place to volunteer for the army all mornin'."

Moses peered closely at Zack. "I don't reckon you to be of age yet, Zack Boone. How old are you?"

Zack stood tall. "I can't rightly be sure, since my old granny raised me after my folks died. She said her figurin' might be off and she never was certain. The way she put it, I'd be about twelve now. Only I'm guessin' it's more like fourteen."

Moses grinned. "I believe your granny's got a lot more wisdom than you be givin' her credit for. Not to say there ain't some drummer boys and officer's boys might be near your age in the army."

"Granny died last spring," Zack stated, "so I guess nobody knows for sure how old I be." Quickly he filled Moses in on his visit to the city with Ben and his folks. "So I guess it's time I was leavin'," he said.

Moses lifted Zack's chin. "You listen good now, son. The army is no place for running away to 'less you plan to work and work hard. Once you put on that uniform the army be ownin' all there is of you." His eyes searched Zack's. "A black soldier in the United States army has to be the best so our people can be proud. That means he has to be willing to dig ditches or whatever else the army wants done. Maybe when you get a mite older you can be a soldier." Zack's heart sank, and he lowered his eyes.

The soldier moved his hand to Zack's shoulder. "Course, if you was to join as a drummer boy you'd be wearin' army clothes, eatin' army beef, drawin' pay, and could help out the chaplain too. Chaplain Turner's been asking the army for an assistant all along. If your heart is set on helpin', maybe you best be talkin' to the chaplain."

A slow smile spread across Zack's face. "I was plannin' on being a drummer boy if the army would have me, and helpin' Chaplain Turner would sure be great." He didn't mention the fact that so far he had never even tried to play a drum.

"The Reverend Turner is chaplain of the First United States Colored Infantry," Moses said. "That's my outfit, and we'll be pullin' out for Virginia any time. Right now the chaplain is signing up volunteers down at the recruiting office, but I can't promise anythin'. If you still want to come, that's where I'm headin'."

"I'd be sure pleased to go with you," Zack said. He stood as tall as he could.

"Well, then," Moses said, "first thing we need to do is see Chaplain Turner." With his arm on Zack's shoulder he directed the way toward the army's recruitment station for black soldiers.

Inside the small building with the sign printed in large letters, BUREAU FOR COLORED TROOPS, Moses left Zack seated in the waiting room. Zack hardly dared breathe when the door to the inner office finally opened.

"Go on in," Moses said, motioning to Zack. "The chaplain wants to see you."

Zack looked at Moses. "You comin'?" he asked hopefully.

"Ain't me he's wantin' to see." Moses grinned and stepped aside. Taking a deep breath, Zack entered the room and stood quietly. He recognized the chaplain at once.

Seated behind a table Chaplain Turner looked stern as his black eyes searched Zack's. His broad dark face was clean shaven, showing a strong square jaw. He sat straight, almost rigid. "So you are the lad Private Comstead thinks he's found for me. Can you read and write, young man?"

"Yes, sir," Zack managed to say.

"So you can read and write. That interests me very much. Sit down," the chaplain commanded and pointed to a chair near Zack. "Now, suppose you tell me where you come from and what it is you want with the army."

Zack swallowed hard and began. "My ma and pa died of the fever before I was a year old. My granny brought me up. Granny used to help out sometimes at the Reverend Stewart Able's place." At the mention of Ben's father the chaplain raised his eyebrows.

"I reckon you know Reverend Able," Zack said. "He was one of the speakers at the Cooper Union meeting on New Years Day." The chaplain nodded. "I was there," Zack said proudly. "Anyways, Ben Able and me kind of growed up together. His folks treated me like kin. They brought me with them to visit New York City. Only Ben's folks won't be goin' back to Tarrytown no more, and I figure it's time I head out on my own. And like you said at the rally, this war is our people's war." A strong feeling swept over him the way it had that night at Cooper Union Hall when the chaplain called for blacks everywhere to rise up in support of the

Union and join the fight to free their brothers. But all he could say was, "I want to join up."

Chaplain Turner looked thoughtful. "Did you tell Reverend Able about your plans?" he asked.

Zack could feel his face burning. "No, sir. Ben said he would tell his pa tonight. Guess I knew it wouldn't be no easier which way I did it." Zack's throat felt dry. No matter how he said it, he had left without taking leave of Ben's father.

The chaplain said nothing for a moment. "Tell me, son, how did you learn to read and write?"

Zack looked up eagerly. "Mistress Capp, sir. I been doin' chores for her back in Tarrytown. Ain't anybody Mistress Capp can't teach to read and write. Used to be a schoolteacher before she got too old."

Chaplain Turner chuckled. "A lot of men who walk in here can barely sign their own name," he said. "I plan to change that. Every man who wants to learn ought to have that chance." The chaplain paused. His eyes seemed far away. "I can use a boy who reads and writes. It may be the Lord's way for both of us. I will have to notify Reverend Able, you understand?" Zack could only nod in agreement.

Reverend Turner looked down once more at a form in front of him. "Age? Private Comstead says your grandmother raised you, but you believe you are older than she thought?"

"Yes, sir," Zack said and explained about his grandmother's poor memory.

"You are not old enough to be a soldier." The chaplain laid down his pen. "I could hire you as my helper and pay you myself. Many of the officers have boys who are not in the army but work as servants for them. On the other hand, if you are bent on joining this army properly, how would you like to be a drummer boy? In your spare time I could use you to help with the men's schooling."

Zack wanted to shout, but he carefully said, "Yes, sir, that would be fine."

Chaplain Turner scribbled something and went on. "Next of kin?"

"Guess that would be my old Uncle Uriah," Zack replied.

Quickly Zack explained that his uncle had no need of him. The chaplain continued to ask questions and write down Zack's answers. "Well now, that seems to be all we need. You wait here, young man."

Zack swallowed hard and sat rigid on the wooden chair waiting for the final word to come. When Chaplain Turner returned he smiled and laid a paper in front of Zack. "Sign here, son." Carefully Zack signed his name where the chaplain pointed.

Chaplain Turner scribbled something on a paper, folded it, and handed it to Zack. "Take this and have Private Comstead show you where to go Soon as the *Nantucket* is ready to sail we leave for Virginia. Welcome aboard, son." A smile lit the chaplain's face, softening its features, as he held out his hand. Zack grasped his hand. He barely heard the rest of the chaplain's words. An hour later he was a drummer boy in the Union army and assistant to Chaplain Turner.

At the docks the *Nantucket* floated on the water like a huge dark bird. Awed by the giant steamship, Zack stared at its wheels, its guns, its great coils of rope, and its long decks. Down in the hold he found a seat in a corner between Moses and another soldier. The warm air smelled of food and the odors of bodies crowded together. Everywhere Zack looked men sat or sprawled.

"What you be doing here, boy?" The soldier who spoke sat a few feet away. He face was thin, his eyes red and watery. "You ain't old enough to leave your mama's skirts," he said.

"Leave him be," Moses warned. "He's a drummer boy and the chaplain's helper." Zack held his head high. He was Chaplain Turner's assistant.

"Rest of us be digging dirt, building bridges, and anything else too hard for white folk." The man sneered as he spoke, then spit. "Only fighting colored men likely to see is from behind a mule wagon."

Next to him an older man spoke out. "Word coming down is that we all be seein' action soon as the weather turns and the army can move men and wagons." Several voices agreed they had heard the same. "Reckon then you be wishin' you was back in New York."

Moses leaned over to Zack. "You don't need to fret none. Chaplain Turner's got the good Lord watching over him. You stick with him and you'll do fine."

"Yes, sir," the older man who had spoken out said. "Seen the chaplain tending the wounded right in the middle of battle. Minié balls flying every which way. Seen one go clear through the top of his hat without hurtin' him none."

Zack tried to picture Chaplain Turner on the battlefield under the fire of enemy rifles shooting the deadly bullets known as minié balls. Zack drew in his breath. He had no idea what a drummer boy or a chaplain's assistant was supposed to do. All he wanted to do was help win the war for freedom. After a while Zack closed his eyes.

When he opened them again it seemed as if a sea of black faces were all around him. The soldier with the red, watery eyes glared at him, and Zack looked away. Some of the men were trying to sleep. Next to him Moses snored gently. Under him the ship moved. One thing was sure, there was no escape now.

3

A Day to Remember

Zack rubbed his cold hands together and blew on them. He picked up his drum sticks and tapped them lightly against the wood of his bunk bed. "Guess I'll be turning these back in with my drum," he said to his roommate, Caleb.

Caleb, two years older than Zack, and a good drummer, tapped lightly on his drum. "I bet in another month you would have been playin' right smart enough," he said.

"I reckon so," he said. For two months he had practiced the difficult drum calls every drummer boy had to learn. In his spare time he helped Chaplain Turner. His head felt crammed with drills and army rules and regulations. At least he wouldn't have to play a drum anymore in his new job with Chaplain Turner. The chaplain's request for a full-time assistant had come through, and he had asked for Zack." Guess I'll miss practicin' with you."

Caleb laughed as he fixed his drum straps over his shoulders. "You ready?"

"Almost," Zack answered. He finished straightening his bunk, folded the woolen army blanket, and placed it carefully at the head. In the army everything had a place, and it had better be there. He pulled the glazed rubber blanket over the foot, just as Sergeant Trask had instructed, and hung his tin cup in place next to his bed. It was a serious offense in the army to lose a cup or plate.

"Too bad you won't be drillin' with us," Caleb said, then grinned.

"I reckon my feet ain't feelin' one bit bad," Zack replied quickly. In a few minutes every drummer boy would beat out the signals for morning drill for his company. Soldiers not on guard duty or sick in the hospital drilled for an hour and a half each morning and two hours each afternoon while the drummers beat the drill commands.

Zack whisked a single piece of straw from the floor. "That one piece could catch old Sergeant Trask's sharp eye," he said. "Next thing you know we both be doing extra chores." The sergeant liked to surprise his men with occasional inspections in addition to the usual Sunday morning ones.

"Guess I won't ever understand what makes the army so particular 'bout a little thing like a piece of straw," Caleb complained. He stooped his tall, lean body and stepped outside. Caleb's skin was a shiny blue-black. Without his cap his hair curled in a tight thin fuzz that made the shape of his head stand out. Zack handed him the forgotten cap. Caleb grinned, and a small scar at the left side of his mouth indented slightly. "Seems like the only thing I don't forget is this here drum." It was true. Caleb was two years older than Zack, the youngest in Company B of the First United States Colored Infantry Regiment until Zack came. He was the best drummer Zack had ever heard and could play almost anything, but outside his music he was downright forgetful. It worried Zack.

"Reckon I won't see you much before tattoo," Zack said. Tattoo was the signal played just after dark for roll call and the ordering of the men to their quarters. "Chaplain Turner's plannin' to visit the men in the hospital as soon as we get through teachin' in the schoolhouse and rounding up recruits on a few farms outside of town."

Caleb nodded. "Sounds as bad as Sergeant Trask," he stated. "That man got more jobs waitin' for a body than fleas on a hound dog."

Zack grinned. "That's army life, and speakin' of jobs, we best be movin' on."

Caleb swung into an easy stride alongside Zack. "Leastwise, Sergeant Trask ain't mean." Caleb gave a shiver as he spoke. "Sergeant Dole is meaner than a weasel when he drills us. Don't matter how good I play. I can't please that man." Caleb rubbed his left ear. "This ear still feels like I got cotton stuffed in it ever since Trask boxed it good 'cause I wasn't playin' to suit him. Yesterday while we were marchin' he knocked Moses over the head for being too slow in the march. It's plain he is one white man who don't like colored folk. I 'spect I'm gonna be in trouble till that man can't find no more excuses for bein' mean, and that don't look like any time soon." Company B was an all-Black unit as was the regiment of the First United States Colored Infantry. Though a few of the officers over the colored troops were blacks like Sergeant Trask, most of the officers were white men. Above the rank of sergeant there were no black officers.

The thought of someone striking Moses made Zack grit his teeth. It was against the army's rules for an officer to mistreat his men. Something should be done about it.

At the chaplain's hut Caleb left Zack and went on his way whistling. As Zack entered, the Reverend Turner looked up from the wooden box he used for a desk and nodded. His broad forehead wrinkled with a light frown. Like Caleb's, the chaplain's close-cropped black hair revealed a well-shaped head and, like Caleb's, his skin was dark. Chaplain Turner stared into space briefly then returned to the work in front of him. Zack knew better than to interrupt him. For the next several minutes he worked quickly and quietly setting the chaplain's things in order.

"That should do," Chaplain Turner stated. "Reports and more reports. I ought to teach you, Zack, how to fill out these things so I can use my time for the Lord's work." He leaned back, sighed, stretched his arms, then stood. "You bundled up good, son? Seems like our people just can't take this cold. The men coughed so bad on dress parade yesterday that the captain ordered them all dosed with cough syrup before parade from now on." Zack grinned. The sweet syrup would not be all that unwelcome.

The morning passed quickly for Zack. As he followed the chaplain on a visit to an outlying farm, a half-dozen barefooted children swarmed out into the cold to greet them. Their ragged clothes were far too thin for early spring. From his coat pocket the chaplain took a handful of hard candy and gave it to the children, beginning with the youngest child. Zack knew he bought the candy with his own money from one of the camp sutlers, peddlers who sold the men all kinds of things the army didn't provide. The children scampered back inside the wooden cabin that to Zack looked more like a shanty than a cabin.

A woman wrapped in a shawl came to the door. "That you, Massa Turner?" she called. "You come on in now. Jeff be right glad soon as he come."

Chaplain Turner stepped inside, and Zack followed. Like the others they had visited, the cabin was small, dark, and smoky. A rag covered its one window. Zack saw no furniture besides a broken table. The children sat on reed mats near the fireplace, where a kettle steamed above the hearth. Zack caught the faint smell of pork fat and something else he could not identify.

"Well, Cleo, has your man made up his mind to join the army?" Chaplain Turner asked in a cheerful voice.

"Can't say yet," she replied. "Long as the army give him work to do we get along. He say if he join the army colored soldiers don't get paid same as white ones. White soldier gets thirteen dollars a month and three-fifty more for his clothes. Black soldiers get ten dollars a month, and they takes three dollars out for his clothes. Jeff say it ain't right."

Chaplain Turner nodded. "Get the same ten dollars a month myself," he said. "But I can promise you, Cleo, that friends in high places in Washington are at work on behalf of our men. Before this year is up our soldiers will have their pay raised equal to whites." The chaplain's voice was confident.

Cleo looked at him and shook her head. "Long as my Jeff's workin' for the army we doin' alright."

"I'm afraid that is all done for now, Cleo." Gently Chaplain Turner explained. "Jeff won't be gettin' any more work from the army unless he joins up. The new law says the army can't hire a man who is between the ages of eighteen and forty-five if he is able bodied enough to be a soldier."

"My Jeff be mighty strong," Cleo said slowly. "But there ain't nothin' left 'round here for him to do if he done lose his work for the army."

"That's right," the chaplain agreed. He looked at the children. "I fear joining the army is Jeff's best choice if these children are to have food this winter. Once Jeff joins, you and the children as the family of a colored soldier can get help from the government's Superintendent of Negro Affairs. You just ask me, and Zack here will write a letter to the superintendent for you."

Cleo looked at Zack curiously. "You be young to be writin'," she said. Her dark eyes were full of trouble as she turned back to the chaplain. "Maybe you be right."

"Cleo, there's something else I'm needing to warn you and Jeff about. The government tells every state in the Union how many men they have to send into the army. Some of the northern states are hiring men called recruiters to find volunteers. They pay a bounty for every Negro the recruiters bring in to take the place of a northern man. Some of those recruiters are working here in Virginia in Union-occupied territory to find men."

Chaplain Turner looked grim. "It won't be safe for men like Jeff. These men aren't above carting off black men and forcing them to sign up for the army and then pocketing the money that belongs to the men for signing up." Chaplain Turner patted Cleo's arm. "I don't want to see any harm come to your Jeff."

The chaplain turned to go. "You tell Jeff the best thing he can do is come see me. I'll help him join up and see that it's done properly. You and the children will be glad for the money the government pays for signing up."

When they had left the cabin behind, Zack asked, "You reckon Jeff will join up?"

Chaplain Turner looked thoughtful. "If the recruiters don't get to him first. They want their money, and they don't care how they get it. Most of the time they show a paper to a fellow who can't read or write and tell him the government says he has to go along with them." The chaplain scowled at Zack. "Those of us who can read and write have got to pass on the tools of learning, son."

"Yes, sir." Reverend Turner ran a school for the men who wanted to learn to read and write. Only this morning Zack had helped unpack a load of books that had been sent to the chaplain from a church up north.

The large canvas-tent schoolhouse near the edge of camp was packed. "You got a spelling book for me?" a dozen voices asked at once. Eager hands reached for the books Zack carried.

"Beginners go with my assistant," Chaplain Turner commanded. "The rest of you gather 'round over here. And don't you fret, those of you who don't have a book," he added. "We've been promised another load of spelling books and primers from the good folks back home." A thunder of glad hand clapping and shouts of "Thank the good Lord" followed his announcement.

In the large group around Zack a familiar face caught his eye. It was Moses. Surprise caught Zack before he could hide it from the young man's gaze. A look of understanding passed over Moses' face. "Now don't you feel bad," he said, "just 'cause I ain't learned to read yet. You do your stuff and make us all proud."

One older man spoke quietly. "The Lord done chose you, boy, when he give you a head start so as you can help the rest of us catch up."

Zack's throat felt dry, and for a second he couldn't speak. Then, holding his primer as if it were a live thing about to jump out of his hands, he began. "The first thing we got to do is learn the letters." A chorus of "That's right, brother" urged him on. The lesson went well. As he finished, Zack looked up to see Chaplain Turner, who had been quietly listening, smile broadly at him.

It was late by the time they arrived at the hospital. An old, red brick two-story building that had once been a factory served as the hospital. A soldier stood quard at its wide wooden door. "Nobody allowed in after hours," he said as Chaplain Turner and Zack approached.

"Chaplain Turner, here to see my men from the First United States Colored Troops, sir. And this is my assistant. Now please let us in."

The guard did not budge. He looked briefly at the two. "Don't look like no chaplain to me. Seeing as how you ain't no surgeon, and that ain't no officer's uniform, you can't go in. I got my orders not to let anyone in after hours."

Anger rose in Zack. The white soldier showed no respect for Chaplain Turner's word.

Reverend Turner's voice was like steel. "How I look makes no difference. I am a chaplain and an officer. A chaplain is free to come and go anytime to visit the sick or wounded in his regiment. I insist you step aside." The look on Chaplain Turner's face was fierce.

The guard scowled. "You say you're a chaplain. You got proof?" The man spit and stared past the chaplain as if he were no longer there. It was more than Zack could bear. He could feel his face burning.

Chaplain Turner calmly withdrew a paper from his pocket and handed it to the soldier. "It is true, sir, that the army has not yet issued us chaplain's uniforms. I should think you would have noticed that by now. However, sir, this order will make it plain who I am."

The man took the paper and looked at it without lowering his gun. His lips formed the words as he read silently. Roughly he shoved the paper back at the chaplain and stood aside from the door to let them pass. Zack refused to look at the man as he followed Chaplain Turner inside.

In the Negro ward Zack greeted the men he knew and nodded to others. The sound of coughing filled the ward. Many of the men were down with fevers, and some with pneumonia. While the chaplain visited, Zack made his way to the bedside of one of the young officer's boys down with pneumonia. "How you doin', Joshua?" Zack asked.

The boy's dark face had a gray pallor, and his eyes seemed too bright as he turned toward Zack. "Guess I be doin' good," he whispered. A deep cough racked him, and Zack quickly lifted his head and doubled the pillow under him. "Thanks,"

Joshua said. "Don't like missin' all the fun layin' in here."

"Missin' work you mean," Zack teased. Joshua coughed, and Zack patted his shoulder. "Better let you rest," he said. Joshua nodded and closed his eyes. Zack pulled the blanket higher on the boy's chest and quietly left.

It had been a long day, and Zack was tired. He was glad when at last the chaplain left the hospital. As they walked outside, the drum call sounded to signal evening dress parade. An officer hurrying past recognized Chaplain Turner and shouted: "To your place, man. The president is coming!"

"Hurry, boy," Chaplain Turner ordered. A look of pure astonishment covered his face. The two of them ran toward the parade grounds.

"Attention!" The commanding officer barked the order, and every man in the outfit stood stiff and straight, including Zack. He ignored the drops of sweat running down his face. The president of the United States, Mr. Lincoln, was coming.

Down between the rows of men the president came, flanked on his right by men in top hats and dark suits, and on his left by the general and other high-ranking officers. The president stood head and shoulders taller than the rest. His dark beard and black suit made him appear even taller. As Mr. Lincoln passed he looked at Zack. His face above the beard was deeply lined and weary, but his eyes were kind and gentle. His mouth lifted at the corners into a brief smile at Zack. Then he was gone.

Zack had almost forgotten to breathe he was so overcome by the sight of the president, the great man who had signed the law to free the slaves.

Tears glittered in Chaplain Turner's eyes. "We've been blessed, son," he said to Zack. "This moment is one you won't ever forget."

Back in his hut Zack still had time before tattoo to do one thing. Taking out his writing materials he began a letter. "Dear Ben, . . ." He stopped to search for the right words. He wanted to tell it right, especially the part where the president smiled at him. He finished writing, sealed the letter, and set it in his pack as tattoo sounded.

As the sergeant began roll call, a breathless Caleb slipped into place next to Zack. When the men were dismissed to their quarters, Caleb grinned. "Forgot something. Had to go back for my cap." Zack shook his head. One of these days Caleb would get himself in real trouble, and he already had more than enough trouble with Sergeant Dole.

4

Smallpox

In the morning, after Caleb had left, Zack headed for Chaplain Turner's quarters. No one was there. The bed covers were tossed about as if the chaplain had left in a hurry. Zack began straightening things according to army regulations. As he hung the chaplain's tin cup in place Sergeant Trask entered.

The sergeant's large frame seemed to fill the hut. He stood towering over Zack. Trask's dark hair curled close to his head in true African fashion, and his skin was as dark as most of the men's in Company B. Zack feared the man but admired him fiercely. Trask was a Negro officer! He could be as tough as he liked, but the men were proud of him all the same.

"The chaplain's down sick," Trask said. "It looks like smallpox. You feeling okay?" He peered at Zack as if searching for signs of the dread disease.

"Smallpox!" Zack exclaimed. "But he was fine yesterday. Worked himself to the bone and never complained once."

"Sounds just like the reverend to me," Trask stated. "Don't make no difference, 'cause this morning he is covered with bad looking pox sure as you're standing here. Which won't be long. You get yourself over to the hospital on the double for a vaccination. After that the reverend wants to see you. And if he don't have enough work laid up for you, I got plenty." Trask drew his brows together in an attempt to look hard, but the gleam in his eyes and the small twitch of a smile around his mouth betrayed him. Zack saluted smartly.

At the hospital long lines of men waited their turn to be vaccinated. Already a half dozen men had come down with the smallpox. When it was Zack's turn he shut his eyes till the doctor had finished. "That ought to keep you safe, boy," the doctor said. "You think you can keep your eyes open in a real battle?"

Warmth rushed to Zack's face. "Yes, sir. I mean I hope so, sir." The surgeon laughed. "You just better hold on to the reverend's coattails when those guns start whizzing overhead." He dismissed Zack and turned to the next in line. Zack bit his lip. He had let this doctor see his fear of a little thing like a needle. Maybe he would run when a battle came; what then? What if they had a battle now with the Reverend Turner sick? The question brought a cold sweat to Zack as he headed toward the colored ward. Without Chaplain Turner he wouldn't know what to do.

Chaplain Turner looked terrible. Gray skin surrounded the angry pocks broken out all over his face and arms. "Bring me water, son," he whispered.

Zack fetched the water and waited while the man drank. "Thank you. That's better," Reverend Turner said. "I need you to take care of the reports on my desk. You bring them here, and I'll tell you what to write. After that I want you to ride out to Jeff and Cleo's place and tell them he's got to come in now. And one thing more." He looked long at Zack as if to make up his mind about something. "I want you to take on the school by yourself for a time. I know you can do it, son."

"Don't fret yourself none," Zack said. Inside his stomach jumped. To help Chaplain Turner was one thing, but to walk into the school by himself and teach grown men was another. But the chaplain was too sick now to argue with him. "Just you get well, sir," Zack said. There was something Zack wanted desperately to ask about, but he didn't dare. He stood hesitating. Chaplain Turner looked at him questioningly. "Your horse, sir," Zack stammered, "do you want me to exercise her for you?"

A hint of a smile creased the chaplain's mouth. "Glad you thought of her, son. When you come back I'll dictate a note for you to take to the stables. Now let me rest." Reverend Turner closed his eyes, and Zack tiptoed out of the ward. Shadow, the chaplain's horse, was the finest chestnut mare Zack had ever set eyes on. For as long as he could remember, Zack had loved horses. He couldn't explain it, but somehow the animals seemed to know he meant them no harm. He had never known a horse he couldn't handle. If he exercised Shadow outside camp maybe he could ride her some. The thought made him forget everything else.

As the morning wore on, the chaplain looked sicker, and his voice grew weaker. "That's all, son, for now," he said motioning Zack to take away the papers. "You'll find some sugar in my pack for Shadow." With those words the reverend once more closed his eyes, and Zack left.

With the sugar wrapped in a paper packet, Zack went straight to the stables. The old man in charge read Chaplain Turner's note while Zack fed Shadow and patted her sleek side. "Looks like the chaplain wants you to ride his horse while he's laid up. Can't hurt the horse none to get her exercise. You'll have to saddle her up yourself, boy, and take care of her when you're through running errands."

Zack stared at the man. Had he heard him right? "Saddle's over there," the man pointed, and Zack nodded dumbly. Chaplain Turner had done more than given Zack permission to exercise Shadow. He was going to ride her for the next few days! As he led Shadow out into the cold air, the older man thrust the chaplain's note into Zack's hand. "Better keep that with you just in case someone challenges you, boy. Can't say I understand the chaplain allowing you to take the horse, but it's his horse, and he can do what he wants with it."

Zack waited until they were outside the camp before he mounted Shadow. For a little while he let Shadow run to ease off her need to exercise. Then he pulled her into an easy trot. No sense getting to

Jeff and Cleo's place too soon. He wanted to enjoy every minute of this ride. He straightened his back and sat tall in the saddle. Few horses could match Shadow's strength and beauty. She was a queen among horses, and Zack felt she somehow knew it.

At the cabin he reined in and called. He expected the children to come running before he dismounted. They ought to enjoy the sight of him riding Shadow. When no one came he climbed down and tied the reins to a stump. "Hello in there," he hollered again. The cabin door opened a crack as he approached, and a girl of about eight looked out. She spoke to someone behind her then opened the door wide for Zack.

"Massa Zack, they done took my Jeff," Cleo cried. Her eyes were red with crying. The smaller children clung to her skirts in fear. "They come here, and the man say he got a paper from the government to take my Jeff for the United States Army." Her voice shook. "Jeff say he can't go now, but they say he got to come right away. The man tell him the government goin' to pay good money. Jeff don't believe that man. He say he ain't goin', and we un's hold on to him, but they just drag him away from us. Don't know where they takin' him, Massa Zack." Cleo hid her face in her hands and moaned.

Zack felt a cold shiver run down his back. "When did they take Jeff?" he asked. He dreaded the answer.

"Must be 'bout an hour ago," Cleo answered. "They was two of them, the recruiter one and his helper. Put my Jeff in the back of their wagon and off they went. What I gonna do now, Massa Zack?"

Zack had no idea. If only he had come earlier maybe he could have saved Jeff. Now what? The room was cold. The fire had died out, and as far as Zack could see there was nothing in the kettle. "You reckon you and the children could put up over at the Dilson place?" he asked.

Cleo pressed the youngest child to her. "Can't stay here with no work and no money comin' in. Best go see Miss Dilson. Ain't nobody gonna bother takin' old Mr. Dilson away."

The Dilsons lived in a cabin similar to Jeff and Cleo's about two miles down the road. Zack hoisted the youngest children onto Shadow and led the sad little party away toward their neighbors.

Mr. Dilson, an old man bent and almost blind, listened to Cleo's tearful story. "You un's come on in by the fire," he said pointing with his cane. "Ain't right takin' folks away like that. Lacey be at work, but she be wantin' you all to stay. Reckon we can put you up for a spell."

Before he left, Zack promised to come back with any news of Jeff. "Don't you fret," he said to Cleo. "Soon as you hear from Jeff I can write a letter for you to the Superintendent of Negro Affairs so you can get some help."

"You keep an eye out for my Jeff, Massa Zack," Cleo begged. Zack promised.

The cold bit into him as he mounted Shadow. It would be good to get back to camp. Maybe Moses or some of the other men could help him figure out what to do about Jeff—if there was anything anyone could do. Caleb would be back by now. Like a jolt it hit him. He had forgotten Caleb's trouble.

Why did the chaplain have to be sick right when they needed him? Zack's stomach rumbled. He was tired and hungry. There was nothing he could do about Sergeant Dole. And who would help Jeff now? The sudden thought that the recruiter who took Jeff might still be nearby startled Zack. The road ahead stretched empty, and with an anxious look behind him Zack urged Shadow to a run.

5

Trouble

At the door to the hospital a guard barred Zack's way. "Too late to see the chaplain," he said. "Transferred him this afternoon to the army hospital in Washington." Zack stared at the man. What had happened? "Get along with you now," the soldier ordered. "You can't come in here."

Bewildered Zack turned away. How could he let Chaplain Turner know about Jeff? What was he supposed to do now? Maybe the reverend had taken a turn for the worse. Fear gripped him. If he died what would happen to Zack? Would they make him go back to being a drummer boy? He could end up like Caleb under a Sergeant Dole. Reverend Turner just had to get better. "Lord," he prayed with his voice choking, "please heal him. Please don't let him die."

For the next hour he worked in the stable. It was the one place he felt safe, sure of himself. Shadow moved impatiently as he rubbed down her sleek sides. "Steady, girl," he coaxed. A sudden blocking of his light made him look up.

It was Sergeant Trask. "Been looking for you, young man. Reckon you won't be riding that horse anymore." Fear shot through Zack. Something must have happened to Chaplain Turner.

"The Reverend Turner is a mighty sick man," the sergeant said. "The army is sending him back to the hospital in Washington until he gets better. This horse belongs to the army now. Leastwise till the reverend gets back, and I don't 'spect we'll see him before summer's end, from what I hear. You listenin', boy?"

"Yes, sir," Zack answered. Everything seemed to be happening at once. Caleb could lose his hearing if Dole kept on striking him, and there was Jeff, and now the chaplain. Sergeant Trask smiled. "Don't fret none about the reverend. He's tough as hide." The sergeant cleared his throat. "Looks like you gonna be officer's boy to that young white officer from Massachusetts, Captain Hale."

Zack stared in astonishment at Trask. "What about Chaplain Turner's work?" he asked. "And the men's schoolin'?"

"Ain't nobody takin' the chaplain's place, far as I know. As to the schoolin', I reckon what you do on your own time is your business, so long as you don't break no army rules. One thing more; you can stay on with Caleb. Captain Hale says you might as well stay put, since he 'spects he'll have to give you back to the reverend once he is better. Hale won't be back for two days. Meanwhile, I got plenty for you to do." Zack felt like groaning but he didn't dare. Without the chaplain to give orders and keep the men in line, they'd just have to call off the school. Meanwhile, till the reverend came back the men could study on their own.

At school the talk was mostly about Chaplain Turner. Zack hadn't yet mentioned closing the school till the chaplain was better. It was Moses who put Zack on the spot. "I reckon you are the teacher, boy," Moses said. "Chaplain Turner will be countin' on us to go right on with our learnin'." He looked expectantly at Zack.

Zack could feel the eyes of the men in the room looking at him. Not two feet away sat the sullen-faced soldier who had told him to go back to his mama the first time they had met. His grin had lost none of its sneer as he caught Zack's eye. But there were others like Moses looking at him, and Zack made up his mind. "Guess we ought to carry on the way the reverend would want us to," he said. For the next hour Zack set the men to studying and worked with small groups. The lesson was over before he remembered Jeff and Cleo's problem.

"Moses," Zack called across the room as he got up. "You know anythin' about those recruiters from the north who took Jeff Combs away earlier today?" There was a sudden hush around him. Most of the men knew Jeff.

"Who took Jeff?" Moses demanded. Zack told what had happened. Moses shook his head. "No tellin' where they took him. For certain sure, they won't be bringin' him here. The colonel wouldn't stand by and allow a man to be forced into signing up like that."

A soldier named Abraham spoke up. "Might be taking him to Craney Island." Abraham rolled back his sleeves and held up his arms. Deep scars circled both wrists. "Got these at Craney. On my way to work in the field one morning two white men come shoving a paper at me and sayin' they got orders to take strong colored men like me into the army. I didn't want to go and leave my family, but they made me. The white colonel at Craney put me in the guardhouse 'cause I wouldn't sign up for the army. I had to walk around with a fifty-pound iron ball on short chains 'round my wrists. When I couldn't hold it no more the chains just yank into my flesh. I signed up." He paused and pulled down his sleeves. "Lucky for me I got sent here."

Moses held up his hand for silence. "We don't know where Jeff is at. I reckon right now the only thing we can do for Jeff is take a collection for his family." He held out his cap. The men took the hat and passed it solemnly. Zack put in all the coins he had in his pocket.

Moses handed the money to Zack. "Since Jeff's family is stayin' at the Dilsons' place, Miss Dilson can take this money to them. She'll be working right now doing officers' laundry."

Three women were working on the laundry. Zack watched as a tall black woman finished taking clothes from the line. The woman's face was surprisingly young as she turned to Zack. "You want somethin'?" she asked.

Zack flushed. "I'm lookin' for Miss Dilson," he stammered.

"I reckon you talkin' to her." The woman's dark eyes sparkled with laughter. She had not yet heard about Jeff and his family. She had been at the laundry all day and didn't know Cleo and the children were at her father's place. "That ain't right to go takin' a good man off like that," she said as Zack finished.

The other women came to hear about Jeff and added their words of sympathy for the poor family. "No tellin' where them recruiters will strike next," said one.

An idea struck Zack. "If you all spread the word, maybe somebody saw which way they were headed." The women nodded in agreement. Miss Dilson promised to see that Cleo got the money from the men, and Zack left. He had no idea what he could do even if they did find out where Jeff was.

The following morning, April first, turned warm and sunny. At six A.M. Zack stood in line for roll call. Sergeant Trask called the roll and then dismissed the men. Zack still had thirty minutes before breakfast, and he had already cleaned up his quarters.

A soft wind blew against his face as he walked toward the stable. In his hand he clutched a small paper of sugar for Shadow. No matter who rode Chaplain Turner's horse now, Zack would see to it that she had her sugar as long as he could. He sighed. Everything was changed with the chaplain gone. Part of Zack wanted to be in the army and part of him wanted to be home even if it meant working for Mistress Capp. What if Captain Hale turned out to be as mean as Sergeant Dole, the Weasel? Could he stand it?

"Massa Zack, over here." It was Miss Dilson beckoning to him from behind the company cook house. "We got the word," she said as Zack approached. Her eyes sparkled with excitement. "Them recruiters that took Jeff ain't left yet. They done stopped at three other farms out a piece. Liza's mama saw the wagon with Jeff in it while she was callin' on Granny T, who lives back of the old Bell place. They was headin' down the road that goes by Merton's farm about the time Liza's mama was comin' home. She say that be just 'fore dark. Ain't nothin' else down there but the woods and Merton's place."

"You think they might still be there?" Zack asked. It was not yet six-thirty.

"Can't say," Miss Dilson answered. "If they spent the night, they might be. What you thinkin to do?"

Up till now Zack had no idea of what to do. If Jeff was in that wagon maybe there was a way to get him out. Only how could he get there in time? His hand closed tightly around the packet of sugar. Shadow. If he could ride Shadow maybe he could do something to help Jeff. In his pocket was the paper from Chaplain Turner giving him permission to ride Shadow.

"Miss Dilson, can you ride a horse?" Zack blurted out. "You can ride behind me and hold on.

If we go right now there is still a chance we can find Jeff."

Miss Dilson stared at Zack as if he had lost his mind. All at once her face broke into a smile. "Don't nobody own me no more. I can come and I can go if I want. All the same, I got to be back here to do that laundry 'fore this mornin' is over."

"Then we better get goin'," Zack ordered. He could miss breakfast, but after that he was supposed to report to Sergeant Trask. Sweat poured down his back as he headed for the stable. He didn't dare tell Miss Dilson that what he was about to do could land him in the guardhouse.

6

A Wild Rescue

Shadow neighed her gladness as Zack fed her the sugar. The guard who had seen him go out on Shadow the day before nodded as Zack rode past. Miss Dilson was waiting outside the camp down the road a way. When Zack stopped to help her mount behind him, Shadow seemed to understand and gave them no trouble. Miss Dilson held tight to Zack's waist as he raced Shadow away from camp. Neither of them spoke except when Miss Dilson pointed out the way to Merton's farm.

At the entrance of the road into the woods Zack stopped and led Shadow off the road. "You wait here while I take a look," he ordered. Zack kept to the woods until he could see the small frame house. In front was the wagon! The dark figure in back had to be Jeff. He was surely tied up or he would have run off long ago. Smoke curled from the chimney of the house. The men were probably still eating breakfast. Whatever he did, it had to be done soon. But what could he do? Miss Dilson was probably shaking back in the woods, and he didn't feel much braver.

"Lord," he whispered, "you know those men have done wrong takin' Jeff like that. But I don't

50

know what to do. Please help us find a way, Lord." Zack stole quickly back to where Miss Dilson waited. One thing he knew for sure—he needed her help.

"They got Jeff in the wagon," he said keeping his voice low. "If we can untie Jeff and get him back to camp before they know what's happened, it could work."

Miss Dilson looked scared, but she spoke firmly. "I know that horse ain't gonna hold three of us, so maybe I just keep runnin' through these woods back to Granny's place down the road."

Zack frowned. "If I ride in there to get Jeff I might not have time to untie him and get him up on Shadow before they come after us. We need something to take their attention away. Now, if I was to sneak in there and untie Jeff and bring him back here the two of you could make it back to camp on Shadow."

Miss Dilson tied her scarf firmly about her head. "Now you listen to me," she ordered. "Soon as you untie Jeff and get him into the woods, someone is gonna drive that there wagon straight down the road in plain sight. That be me. When I get to the end of the road I'll turn away from camp. Then I'll just jump out and let them mules run all they wants to. Nobody gonna see me once I'm in them woods headin' for Granny's place. She hide me good, too."

"It just might work, and we ain't got time to argue," Zack said. "But I don't want those men lookin' for you. You better put on my cap and jacket. That way they'll be lookin' for a tall soldier riding off with their wagon."

Miss Dilson laughed. She was a good deal taller than Zack. Her long arms stuck out of the jacket sleeves. But with the cap on, from the back she would look like a soldier.

"Never goes nowhere without my knife," she said. In her hand was a long-bladed knife that she held out to Zack. "Use it for cuttin' corn and most anything."

"Thanks," Zack said. Together they crept back toward the house. At the edge of the woods he paused, nodded at Miss Dilson, and ran to the back of the wagon. His heart pounded as he climbed into the wagon where a wide-awake Jeff stared at him over the huge gag tied into his mouth. Quickly Zack slit the ropes binding Jeff's feet and then went to work on the ones around his arms. "You got to come quick," he whispered. "There's a horse waitin' in the woods."

Jeff nodded frantically. Then he pulled off his gag as the last rope fell from his wrists. Together they scrambled from the back of the wagon. In his eagerness Zack went first. Too late he saw Jeff stumble.

"It be my legs," Jeff whispered. "Can't hardly make 'em hold me."

Panic whipped through Zack. Any minute the door to the house might open and they would be caught. He bent to help Jeff stand. With a groan Jeff put his arm around Zack and staggered a few steps. "You got to do better than that," Zack urged. Jeff rubbed his legs desperately and tried to run, but all he could do was limp along.

Miss Dilson came running and put her weight under Jeff's other arm. "Come on, man," she whispered, "ain't but a few steps into them woods and freedom." Jeff walked leaning heavily on their supporting shoulders. Miss Dilson began to half drag him. "You got to think runnin', man," she commanded.

Zack felt his stomach lurching. They had to hurry. All at once Jeff seemed to come alive. He was moving faster, almost running. They reached the woods, and finally there was Shadow waiting.

"ᵁu two get on Shadow and ride fast as you can back to camp," Zack said. He and Miss Dilson half pushed Jeff onto Shadow's back. But when Zack went to help Miss Dilson mount she backed away.

"I'm goin' back and get that wagon," she said. Before Zack could stop her she ran through the woods back toward the house.

Zack wanted to stop her but there was no time. With a sob he mounted Shadow. "Run, girl," he whispered in her ear. "Run like the wind." Shadow galloped with all her might. Behind him Zack thought he heard Jeff praying.

They were well down the road when Zack looked back to see the wagon. The mules were racing the wrong way! Miss Dilson was nowhere in sight. In the distance Zack heard rifle shots. He ducked his head low to Shadow's neck and felt the heavy weight of Jeff pressed against his back. With a final burst of speed Shadow flew into camp past the astonished guards. Zack could barely bring her to a stop.

"What is goin' on here?" It was Moses' voice. Company B had guard duty. Between gulps of breath Zack explained. "Get this man to the captain," Moses ordered and motioned to Jeff. "I believe he wants to sign up for the army before some skulkin' recruiters come in claimin' he belongs to them."

"Yes, sir. That's just what I be wantin' to do," Jeff said. "I believes there's a wagon belongin' to them recruiters that's comin' down the road like them mules was wantin' to join up too."

Sure enough, as Zack looked the mules came crashing toward the camp.

Quickly Zack mounted Shadow and turned her toward the wagon. The mules veered to the left to avoid Shadow, and as Zack pressed toward them again they seemed to slow, then with uncertain jerks came to a standstill. One of the guards caught hold of the mules and led them inside the camp as the rest of the soldiers cheered.

Zack patted Shadow and walked her slowly to the stable. Jeff was on his way to sign up. Zack had to rub down the sweating Shadow before he did anything else. He was nearly finished when Sergeant Trask appeared.

"There's two fellows from up north complaining that some tall colored soldier stole their wagon this morning. I don't recall seein' you around this mornin'. Lucky for you that you ain't no tall soldier." The sergeant scratched his head. "Don't know who it might have been. All my men was right here and accounted for, 'cept for you."

Zack kept his eyes down. "Yes, sir."

"I suppose you been takin' leave of the chaplain's horse. She is a mighty fine piece." He patted Shadow's flank firmly. "You got to put her out of your mind, son. She belongs to Captain Hale until the Reverend Turner gets back. Now what is keepin' you? Caleb has been lookin' everywhere for you. Didn't you hear the orders to set up your tents this morning?"

"Yes, sir. I'm goin' right now." Zack hurried away feeling like a weight had rolled from his shoulders. The sergeant was sure to hear about this morning's rescue of Jeff, but by then Jeff would be a new recruit and the men from up north would be gone. They had their wagon back, and besides, they weren't looking for Zack. He wasn't tall enough. That Miss Dilson was sure something.

"Where you been?" Caleb demanded. "This here tent has more buttons than a man can handle by himself." Zack grabbed an end of the canvas and held it while Caleb worked to put the two small tents together. The wooden huts had been good in winter but most of them were infested with lice. The small one-man tents called dog tents could be buttoned together to form one bigger one, and they were clean. "You ain't gonna believe where I been," Zack said softly. Caleb's eyes widened as Zack told of the wild rescue of Jeff.

At the noon dinner Zack ate ravenously. He had eaten nothing since the day before. He had barely finished cleaning his plate when a messenger came looking for him. "The colonel wants you, boy." Zack felt a shiver run down his back.

The way to the colonel's quarters seemed to go on forever. Thoughts of what punishment awaited him made his legs feel weak. He had taken Shadow out without permission. Worse, he had acted like he was on an errand for Chaplain Turner and left camp without permission. Maybe the recruiters knew he was the one who had put Miss Dilson up to stealing the wagon.

Inside a large canvas tent the colonel was seated behind a table. Zack recognized two of the guards from Company B standing near the entry. Jeff Comb stood at one side of the tent and the two rough-looking men next to him. As Zack entered, the two men eyed him with contempt. "He ain't near tall enough to be the one who stole our wagon," one said gruffly.

The colonel raised his hand for silence. "I'll ask the questions here," he said. He looked hard at Zack. "Mr. Comb, is this the young man who rescued you?"

"Yes, sir, that's him," Jeff answered.

The stranger next to Jeff sputtered. "You ain't gonna take the word of no Negro, Colonel. I tell you this boy is lying."

The colonel turned to Zack. "You were Chaplain Turner's assistant, weren't you? Tell me, son, where and in what condition did you find Mr. Comb?"

Zack swallowed hard. "Yes, sir. Jeff, I mean Mr. Comb, was lying in a wagon with his hands and feet tied. The wagon was parked outside Merton's farm."

"What brought you to the Merton's farm?" the colonel asked.

"Well, sir, yesterday mornin' the chaplain ordered me to ride out to Jeff's place and tell him to come in and sign up. When I got there Jeff was already taken off in these men's wagon. Only I didn't know where till Miss Dilson, who does the officers' laundry, said Miss Liza's mama spotted the wagon over toward Merton's place last night. So I went on out there this morning before breakfast, and sure enough, Jeff was in the wagon all tied up in front of Merton's farmhouse."

"He's lying," the man next to Jeff shouted. "If he rode out there on a horse, then who stole our wagon? Or was that tall soldier we seen driving our wagon your partner?"

The colonel pounded on his table for quiet. "I believe I know from Private Comstead, who was on guard duty, the rest of the story." His look at the two men was cold and hard. "Your wagon came in riderless. Probably following this young man's horse back to camp." He held up his hand as the men began to protest. "Silence. Now, young man," he said to Zack, "I understand you have a letter authorizing you to use Chaplain Turner's horse in your duties for the chaplain?"

Zack fumbled in his pocket and brought out the crumpled note. "Yes, sir. It's here."

The colonel read the note and laid it on the table. "This note from Chaplain Turner is no longer good. You understand that with the chaplain on leave you will not use his horse for any further purposes. I believe your new duties are with Captain Hale." Turning to the two strangers he frowned. "As to you, sirs, I suggest that you leave this camp at once. Take your wagon with you and don't let me catch either of you near my men again."

"But this Negro ain't. . . ." the man next to Jeff protested.

The colonel cut him off. "Private Combs signed up as a volunteer freely of his own will this morning." He motioned to the guards. "Escort these men off grounds immediately," he ordered.

"Son, before you go I have something to say to you," the colonel said. "It was a brave thing you did and a foolish one. You might easily have gotten yourself killed or thrown in the wagon along with Private Combs. All the same, I should think the chaplain will be mighty pleased to hear that you carried out so completely his orders to bring your man in. Dismissed."

Outside, Private Jeff Combs hugged Zack in a great bear hug. "I reckon I won't never forget what you done for me." Though he was half-smothered in the big man's embrace, Zack felt good inside.

All day Zack had not seen Caleb. It was late evening when Caleb finally came in. Carefully he stored his drum then sat down on his pallet and loosened his boots while Zack filled him in on the afternoon's events.

"Just wish they could have kidnapped Sergeant Dole," Caleb replied. "The men won't take much more of his meanness. Leastwise tomorrow I don't reckon he will be callin' anybody down. You know how Major Hopkins likes to come 'round the campfires some nights to hear us colored men singin'? We told him if he come to see us marching tomorrow we got a song he ain't heard yet, and he said he would be there. Course, it's a surprise Sergeant Dole don't know nothin' about yet." Caleb smiled broadly.

"Chaplain Turner said the major is a real fine Christian man."

"That's right," Caleb said. "We're countin' on that being the case." He chuckled softly. Zack grinned. Whatever Caleb and the men were cooking up, he hoped it would help them.

7

Officer's Boy

In the morning Zack had a visitor. It was Miss Dilson with several packages. One was wrapped in white cloth. "These here be corncakes from Liza's mama, preserves from Granny, and this here is your jacket and cap." She handed the things to Zack and smiled broadly.

Inside the cloth, Zack's jacket lay neatly folded. Both the jacket and cap had been cleaned. "I thank you kindly," Zack said. "I was hopin' you didn't get hurt none jumpin' off that wagon yesterday."

"I slowed her some before I jumped. Guess I was so scared I never did turn those mules." Zack laughed, and Miss Dilson laughed with him. When she had left, Zack stored his packages back in the tent. "That Miss Dilson is one fine woman," he remarked to a surprised Caleb, then left.

The encounter Zack dreaded had come. He smoothed down his thick curly hair for the third time and inspected his uniform. There was no sense starting off on the wrong foot with his new boss, Captain Hale. No matter how many times he told himself that Chaplain Turner would be coming back, a small voice inside him kept asking, "What if he doesn't come soon enough? What if this new officer turns out to be like Sergeant Dole, the Weasel?" Zack swallowed hard. What did an officer's boy have to do? He didn't even know.

"So, you are my new boy." The voice was soft, and Zack heard the faintest sound of amusement in it. "I have the chaplain to thank for you, and from what I gather, he plans to have you back when he returns. I hope neither of us shall mind the wait."

At least the man knew Zack was the chaplain's assistant. He saluted sharply. "Yes, sir. I mean no, sir." The captain was the picture of a gentleman Union officer in spotless uniform with shining buttons. His boots were polished, and the handle of his sword gleamed. The skin of his face, though it was white, had a healthy glow. His hair and beard were the palest gold Zack had ever seen on a man.

Captain Hale smiled at Zack's confusion. "Never mind, young man, we shall get on so long as you do exactly what I say." He nodded as Zack quickly responded with a hearty "Yes, sir."

"I hear from the stable master that you have a good hand with horses. I will be using Chaplain Turner's horse and shall expect you to keep her in good shape." Zack felt a warm glow inside him at the thought of caring for Shadow once more. "Right now," the captain went on, "I am invited by Major Hopkins to watch a drill. You may accompany me."

Zack would have followed his new boss, but the captain fell into step beside him. Zack stole a sideway look at the man. There were other officers in camp who made it plain that the colored soldiers were to keep their distance except in the line of duty. A few were friendly enough. Of course, officers and enlisted men weren't supposed to be friends according to the army's strict code of behavior. Rules governed everything, Zack thought, from making a bed right up the line.

They were just in time to hear the sergeant give his first command. Already a small group of onlookers had gathered. Among them was Major Hopkins, who came and stood by Captain Hale. Zack moved slowly away from the officers until he was standing a respectful distance away.

Sergeant Dole called the order, "Support arms! Forward, march!" The men under his command were all colored soldiers. Zack knew how meanly the sergeant had treated them from the first. On the field Caleb struck his drum and then began to beat a stirring roll. Astonishment crossed the face of the drill sergeant as the men started to sing.

The song had a marching rhythm to which the men kept pace as they sang and marched. It was a magnificent sound and sight. Like a small but mighty army the men sang:

> Ride in, kind Savior,
> No man can hinder me.
> O, Jesus is a mighty man!
> No man can hinder me.
> We're marching through Virginny fields.
> No man can hinder me.
> O, Satan is a busy man.
> No man can hinder me.

And he has his sword and shield.
No man can hinder me.
O, old Secesh done come and gone!
No man can hinder me.

On and on, verse followed verse as the men did the difficult drills. Zack felt like singing too.

At a pause in the drill Zack heard Major Hopkins call out, "Well done, Sergeant Dole. An excellent means of drill, and a fine example to the rest of us. Good singing, men," he added.

"I don't believe I have heard that one," the captain remarked as he and Zack left the field and headed toward the stables.

"Me neither," Zack said. "But I reckon I know who wrote it." He explained about Caleb and the men's trouble learning the drill, all except for the part about Sergeant Dole's meanness to the men.

"Your Caleb has a good head on his shoulders," Hale said. "Now let's see just how good yours is with a horse who is not only missing her master but is probably wild for a good ride."

Shadow nickered as Zack approached. With one hand stroking her neck Zack whispered words of comfort to her. "You got to show your stuff," he said softly. "I'm countin' on you, Shadow, to behave yourself till the chaplain gets back, you hear?"

The horse nuzzled Zack's arm as if in reply. Though he ached to ride her when she was saddled and ready, Zack handed the reins to Hale. In a few minutes Shadow and her new master took to each other. He only wished it was Chaplain Turner on Shadow.

By evening dress parade Zack knew that an officer's life was as full as the chaplain's had been. Everything had to be polished and in perfect order. Zack kept busy running errands, finding papers, fetching, cleaning, and learning the unending regulations.

"I shall be gone tomorrow," Captain Hale informed Zack. "You will be assigned to one of the supply wagons till I return." As the captain took the jacket Zack offered him he looked deeply into Zack's eyes. "I want you to know that I do not hold with young boys on the battlefield, but as my boy you will be expected to help out behind the lines with the supply wagons during a battle. You will be at least as safe as the supplies, and, pray God, all of us will come through." He put on his jacket and inspected the buttons. "This is a war that could make a whole new life for your people, Zack."

Lights out came while Zack waited eagerly for Caleb's return. An hour after the camp was quiet Caleb had not come. A knot tightened in Zack's stomach. Something told him Caleb was in trouble. What if the Weasel was angry about the surprise the men had pulled at drill? It was Caleb who had written the song.

Stumbling along the edge of the dark parade ground Caleb searched for his hat. He remembered laying it down just after dress parade. With a sigh of relief he found it, picked it up, and slapped it on his head. Before he could turn to go, heavy hands gripped his shoulders from behind. Caleb smelled the strong smell of whiskey as he twisted to face his captor. It was the Weasel, Sergeant Dole!

"What have we got here?" the sergeant demanded. He held tightly to Caleb as a second man stepped from the shadows. Dole pointed to Caleb. "You see this boy? He plays a mighty mean drum, only I don't think he likes me much. That right, boy?" Caleb said nothing.

"You suppose he can march same as he plays the drum?" Dole laughed, and his friend laughed with him. "Let's just see how you do, boy." He let go of Caleb with one hand and smacked the boy's leg hard with the flat of his rifle butt. "Now march."

Caleb jumped as the rifle butt struck his leg. He wanted to run but he didn't dare. "Please, sir, I got to get back," he pleaded.

Dole seemed to explode with anger. "I'll teach you to march," he said and began hitting Caleb first on one leg then the other. "March," he commanded as he beat Caleb's legs in a wild rhythm with the bayonet. Caleb cried out but the sergeant just kept on hitting him faster and faster. When at last he stopped beating Caleb he barked an order. "You march till there ain't a single star in that sky, you hear? Now march."

Near dawn Caleb crawled into the tent. "Can't march no more. Got to wake up for reveille," he mumbled as Zack sat up. Caleb lay where he had fallen in a crumpled heap on his pallet.

"You okay?" Zack whispered. There was no answer. Zack lay awake listening to Caleb's muffled crying. "That Dole bother you?" Zack asked.

Caleb made no answer, and after a while Zack heard his breathing grow quieter. Sergeant Dole must have punished Caleb, probably for springing the surprise marching song on him during the morning drill. Carefully Zack crept to where his friend lay and inched the covers over him.

Something had to be done about Dole. The men wouldn't stand by and see Caleb mistreated. Zack closed his eyes. If the chaplain were here Zack knew he would do something to help Caleb and stop a possible mutiny. But he wasn't here, and the only way to make a complaint about Dole would be through the officer in charge, a white officer. It wasn't likely they would take the part of a black man against a white fellow officer. That could mean trouble for the Company B men who had to work under Dole and his friends.

Chaplain Turner would say the best way to get help was from the top. Of course, the chaplain meant God first and after that from senators and important men with power. Only Zack didn't know any. Caleb groaned in his sleep. Troubled, Zack turned and tossed. It was almost dawn, and he would have to rouse Caleb.

First light streaked the sky as Zack tried to waken Caleb. "Go 'way," Caleb mumbled. Zack kept shaking him. Finally Caleb opened his eyes, blinked, then sat up. "I got to get up," he said. With a cry of pain he rolled onto the tent floor.

"What happened?" Zack demanded to know.

Caleb lay where he was and moaned. "Dole swatted my legs with the butt of his rifle and then he sent me on a punishment march." Caleb bit his lip. "I could feel my legs hurtin' at first, but after a while I don' remember anythin' but how heavy they were."

"Better let me take a look at those legs," Zack said. For a minute he could not figure out what had happened. The cloth of Caleb's uniform seemed stuffed to bursting and would not budge. Caleb groaned, and Zack stopped. "Your legs must be swelled up something fierce."

It was no wonder Caleb cried with pain at every touch. His legs were swollen into two huge shapeless masses of bruised flesh. "Those legs ain't gonna carry you nowhere, nohow till they go down some," Zack stated.

Before he could think what to do next Sergeant Trask came storming into the tent. At first sight of Caleb's legs he bent down to examine them carefully. "How did this happen, son?" he asked gently.

"The butt of Sergeant Dole's rifle, and punishment march," Caleb whispered.

Zack saw the anger on Sergeant Trask's face. "Dole did this to you?" he asked. Caleb nodded as tears seeped from his eyes. "I'm takin' you to the hospital, son," the sergeant said. He covered Caleb with a blanket and lifted the boy in his strong arms.

When Trask had gone with Caleb, Zack slumped onto his pallet. He didn't feel like eating. He didn't feel like cleaning up the tent. He didn't care anymore. What he wanted was to be out of this army and far away. He thought of Ben's last letter. Maybe he would go as far as Minnesota where Ben and his family were planning to live.

8

The Guardhouse

How long Zack sat on his pallet he didn't know. Outside, a heavy rainfall dulled the noises of camp life. After a while Zack stirred. He could think of only one thing to do. He took out his writing things and began: Dear President Lincoln. For a long time he hesitated, trying to think of the right words. Little by little he put down the story of Caleb, of the men, and of Sergeant Dole's mistreatment of them. He wrote of his fears that the men would not stand for much more of Dole's unfair ways, especially when it came to his beating and punishing Caleb. He stated what he knew to be true of the army's rules about officers striking the men under their command and asked if Mr. Lincoln could help. Finished, he laid the letter down to search for an envelope. A sound at the tent door made him spin around.

The grim face of Captain Hale under his dripping cap, and the steel look of his blue eyes sent a stab of fear through Zack. "So, the cat's away and the mouse will play," Hale said. Before Zack could think of an answer, the captain went on. "I find myself unexpectedly back at camp where I supposed to find you at the quartermaster's. You might at least have showed up there before slouching off on army time." He held up his hand to stop Zack from speaking. "There is nothing I want to hear from you, young man. I am not in the habit of being disobeyed by my men or boys."

At that moment Sergeant Trask looked in. "Beg your pardon, sir," he said, saluting the lieutenant.

"Sergeant Trask, I order you to take this boy to the guardhouse. He is to be held there and given bread and water in place of regular meals until I decide what is to be done with him."

"Yes, sir," Sergeant Trask responded. With one large hand on Zack's shoulder he propelled him through the tent door into the pouring rain. Outside, he moved swiftly toward the wooden guardhouse. "Don't know what you did, boy, but if the captain says guardhouse, that's where you go. From the looks of that tent I'd have put you there myself anyway. Now, what did you do?"

Confused and shaken, Zack tried to answer. "I reckon I didn't report to the quartermaster for work this morning. Captain Hale said he was going out on duty for a few days, and I was to help the quartermaster till he got back."

"What got into you, boy?" Trask demanded. "What were you doing all that time after I left?"

"Writin' a letter, I guess," Zack replied meekly.

"Chaplain Turner would tan your hide if he caught you doing a thing like that on army time. You got to learn, boy, same as the rest of us. This is the army." They arrived at the guardhouse, a grim-looking log building set inside a courtyard surrounded by a high wooden fence.

Sergeant Trask explained Captain Hale's orders to the officer in charge. As he turned to go he lifted Zack's chin with one big hand. "You look at me, boy. This army's gonna make a man of you one way or the other. I aim to see that you don't make no more mistakes, you hear?" Zack nodded. He didn't trust himself to speak.

Zack swallowed hard. The officer behind the desk wrote something in the book before him, then looked up at Zack and frowned. "Can't say I'm pleased to have you here, boy. You are a mite young for this sort of place, aren't you? Nevertheless, my orders are to lock you up, so in you go." He nodded his head to a soldier standing at attention. "Take him to the empty cell on block two."

Silently the guard escorted Zack to a small cell and unlocked the door. "Don't know what you did, boy, but looks like you are in big trouble. Leastwise, you ain't in irons." He pushed Zack inside the cell and closed the door. As he locked the door he warned Zack. "If you know what's good for you, you'll keep quiet. Don't cause yourself no more trouble. The captain don't stand for no sass. I'll be back later."

Zack listened to the man's footsteps die away. A cold silence settled around him. Thick wooden walls surrounded him. High above him a small barred window let in the light. He could see little through the opening in the cell door beyond a patch of the wall across from it.

The cell was bare except for a mouldy straw pallet. Zack sat on it crosslegged and put his head in his hands. None of this would have happened if Chaplain Turner had been here. How had it all happened? He never meant to disobey Captain Hale's orders. It was true he had failed to report for duty. Did that make him a deserter? The army shot deserters. A soft groan escaped his lips. He let the tears flow as he thought about his life now and what it might have been if only he had stayed in New York with Ben and his family and even returned to Tarrytown. He had to let Ben know, explain about Caleb and the letter. The letter was still lying in his tent. For all he knew he might never see his tent or the letter again.

With the passing hours the light in his cell faded till he was sitting in semidarkness. In the distance he heard the sounds of the drums calling the men. He had eaten the dry bread brought to him but saved some of the water. He sipped it now and wished it were hot coffee or even hot water. The air in the cell had grown chill. The sound of footsteps and the jangling of keys brought him to his feet.

A guard opened the door and threw Zack a bundle. "Better wrap that blanket around you before you freeze, boy." When the door closed, Zack quickly wrapped himself in the woolen blanket. Gratefully he lay down on the pallet and tried to sleep. He missed his own tent and Caleb's soft snoring. Worse, he missed being out of this army.

On the officers' side of the camp Captain Hale walked briskly away from the colonel's tent. He had done his best to move the colonel to see justice carried out on the man Dole. Anger still seethed through him at the thought of the man's cruelty. A court martial would be none too heavy a punishment for him. "I should like to be here for that," he thought. His orders of transfer to the Shenandoah Valley were in his coat pocket. The rich farms of the Shenandoah Valley in northern Virginia fed the Southern armies of General Robert E. Lee. The valley had to be captured if Lee's supplies were to be cut off. Cavalry men like the captain would play an important role in the capture of the valley. A smile played on the captain's lips. The transfer was not unwelcome.

Outside the guardhouse the captain paused. For a moment he moved to enter, then changed his mind. He would let the boy wait it out. It could not hurt him, and he had, after all, disobeyed orders. A night in the cell and breakfast on bread and water might toughen him up a little. The boy would need that if he was going to make it in a man's army. Turning away, he stuffed Zack's letter into his pocket and made his way back to his quarters.

Though he heard the morning call to rise, Zack lay where he was on his pallet until the guard appeared with his bread and water. There was little to do after that but sit and wait. When a double set of footsteps stopped outside his cell, he stood rigidly waiting for the worst.

It was Captain Hale who entered the cell. Zack and the captain were left alone facing each other. Hale held out a paper toward Zack. "I happened to see this sticking out of your bedroll after you left yesterday. Though I did not know it was a personal letter until I had read part of it, I fear I am guilty of reading your mail." He extended the letter to Zack, who took it. "I understand, son, why you were upset yesterday. Perhaps I should have let you explain, but nevertheless, an order is an order and must be obeyed under the best and worst circumstances." A look of pain flitted across the captain's face. "If you were my own son I would have disciplined you no less." He laid his hand on Zack's shoulder as he spoke, "I am willing to believe you have learned from this. I should like you to continue in your present service as my officer's boy." Zack's heart raced, and a sudden energy poured through him.

Captain Hale seemed to read the expression of relief on Zack's face. "Last night I spoke to Colonel Wentworth. I took the liberty of showing him your letter. Yours was not the first complaint about Sergeant Dole but the most recent. The colonel will not stand for such behavior in his camp. I do not think you or young Caleb or the men will have anything more to fear from Sergeant Dole."

"Thank you, sir," Zack managed to whisper.

The captain looked thoughtful for a moment. "As to your letter, Zack, I must ask you to consider not sending it. The colonel fully understands why you thought you had to go outside the regular army way of handling such complaints. It is true that a man who brings a complaint risks the anger of his superior officers, but in this instance I can assure you that danger is over. I fear your letter to the president could cause considerable stir and prove to be an embarrassment to the army. If you are willing to abide by my judgment, I believe it best in this case for the army to handle its own affairs in an honorable and swift way."

Zack stared at the captain. "I'm sorry, sir. Here." He offered the letter back to Hale. "Take it, sir. I don't want to stir up trouble. And now that you and the colonel have fixed things there's no need."

The captain smiled. "I think your choice at present is the wisest course of action. Now, I have an offer to make you which you may refuse. I have been transferred to the Shenandoah Valley effective at once. The colonel has given permission to take you with me as my officer's boy. Chaplain Turner is not expected back on active duty for several months. I expect by the end of summer my assignment in the valley will be over." He paused for a moment, and Zack felt his thoughts racing. He could go with the captain or he could stay here. Part of him wanted to go; but part of him wanted to stay here and wait quietly till the chaplain got back and took over.

"If you choose to stay until the reverend returns you will be assigned to some other duty, perhaps to another officer. If you decide to come with me, I will write to Chaplain Turner myself to inform him. You are free to go back to your tent now and think it over, Zack."

Zack continued to stare at the captain. The Shenandoah Valley! Excitement surged through him. The captain wanted him. "Don't need no time, sir. If you'll have me I sure would like to come."

Captain Hale held out his hand to Zack. "You will be ready to leave first thing in the morning. And one thing more: I expect my exact orders to be carried out each and every time. Report to me at my quarters within the hour."

"Yes, sir," Zack said saluting smartly. In the yard the sun shone brightly, and Zack felt its warmth chase the chill of the cell from his bones. He was still in the army. Ahead of him lay a new adventure in a new place. There would be good-byes to say and a quick letter to Ben to tell him of his new post. A twinge of pain darkened the moment as he remembered Caleb.

9

The Shenandoah Valley

It was evening before Zack finished the last of the packing for the captain and was through for the day. He still had time to visit Caleb.

"Can't get this rhythm out of my head," Caleb sang as Zack entered the ward. Caleb was sitting up in his hospital bed, and his slender fingers were tapping out a song against the pillow on his lap. "Might as well practice, since the doc says I have to stay off these legs a day or two. I hear you been beddin' down in the guardhouse for a spell." A wide smile lit his face.

Zack explained. "The captain says you won't be needin' to worry anymore about Dole. We'll all be breathin' easier with Dole transferred. Got somethin' else to tell you, too." In a rush of excitement he told Caleb about Captain Hale's orders to report for duty in the Shenandoah Valley. "Looks like I'm goin' too," he said. "The captain reckons it will all be over in the Shenandoah by the end of summer. That's when Chaplain Turner ought to be coming back, too." At the look on Caleb's face Zack quickly reminded him, "You know I'm just on loan. The captain plans to tell Chaplain Turner himself."

Caleb was silent for a minute. "I reckon you got to go. No tellin' what job you might end up with here if you don't." He extended a thin hand to Zack. "Gonna miss you, brother. Won't be the same without you."

Zack clasped his friend's hand hard. "I'll write you. Now don't you forget what I told you. Every mornin' you wake up and make a list in that head of yours for all the things you got to remember, like your cap for one thing." Caleb laughed, and Zack laughed with him. It felt good to laugh. He didn't want Caleb to know how close he was to crying like a baby.

Zack had one thing more he must do. Moses was not in his tent. One of the men from Company B called out to Zack, "You lookin' for Moses, boy? Ought to be comin' off picket duty any time now."

A few minutes later Zack saw him walking slowly past the cook tent. Moses looked tired from his twenty-four-hour picket duty, but he grinned when he saw Zack. "Well, you don't look none the worse for being in the guardhouse. This army is toughening you up, boy."

Zack remembered the day he had run into Moses in New York City. Thanks to Moses, Zack had found Chaplain Turner. "Looks like I'll be leavin' for a spell with Captain Hale," he said. Quickly Zack explained all that had happened. "Guess you and the others will be doin' the school on your own for a while." From his pack Zack took the reader, a gift from the chaplain to him, and held it out. "I want you to have this, Moses. I know you can learn it."

A slow smile softened Moses' face. He took the book, looked at it, and placed it inside his shirt. "I'm gonna miss you, Zack. Don't worry none about the school. By the time you and the chaplain get back I'll be reading this book."

Zack watched him leave then turned to go to his own tent. He took the shortcut behind the cook tent and had nearly reached his darkened tent when a figure blocked his way.

"I reckon you're that little Caleb brat's tentmate, ain't you? You think your kind can get away with ratting on an officer?" The white man who stood leering at him angrily was not Sergeant Dole but a soldier Zack had seen hanging out with Dole. Zack's heart pounded, and his throat was dry. Before he could say anything the man grabbed Zack's arms. "I'll teach you a lesson you won't forget," he threatened. Zack caught the smell of whiskey as the man lifted him from his feet and shook him wildly.

"Drop the boy," a hard voice commanded. The startled soldier let Zack go. The voice was Jeff's. A small group of men from Company B stood in a half circle behind the man. Even in the semidarkness Zack recognized his friends from the school. "You okay, Zack?" Jeff asked.

"I'm okay," Zack answered. "Don't know what I'd be if you all hadn't come along."

The white man backed off as the half circle of men drew closer. "You ain't heard the last of this," he warned.

In a voice hard and cold Jeff said, "If you touch the boy or any of ours, we'll know." It was all he said, but it was enough. The man left, slinking into the shadows without a word.

Zack shook his head. "You men sure do make a fellow feel safe. Reckon he won't be botherin' nobody for a while. How'd you come by like that?"

"Some of us been following you since you left the captain's quarters," Jonas said. "We thought something like this might happen after the colonel took down Sergeant Dole for mistreatin' his men. That man and Dole stick together like two peas in a pod. This one is almost as bad as Dole, except he ain't a sergeant."

Zack felt a lump in his throat. With friends like these he almost didn't want to leave, even with the captain.

That night in the stillness of the camp he turned and tossed on his pallet. Tomorrow's trip kept filling his mind. One minute he thought maybe he should have stayed and waited for the chaplain's return. The next he felt like he couldn't wait to go. He comforted himself with the thought that he would be back. It was sort of like going on leave for a time like Chaplain Turner.

In the morning Zack and Captain Hale boarded the train that was already crowded with soldiers. The captain led the way to their seats. While they rode they talked, and Zack found himself telling

Hale about his life in New York and about Ben and his family.

The captain was a good listener. He laughed at Zack's description of a train ride the boys had taken disguised as Quakers. At the place where Zack spoke of an encounter with a dishonest soldier who had tried to kidnap him, Hale looked serious. "That was a tight situation," he said. "May we all have good friends like that Ben of yours."

Zack thought for a moment. "Yes, sir, but I reckon like Ben's preacher pa says, there's one friend a body can't do without. I promised him if he'd get me out that time I'd sure know it was him that done it."

The captain stared at Zack. "You mean God, don't you?"

"Sure reckon I do," Zack said with a certainty in his voice. Hale said nothing, and for a while the two sat in silence.

As their train lurched across the railroad bridge high above the Potomac River below, Captain Hale pointed to the deep cleft of the triple gorge where the Shenandoah River met up with the Potomac's waters. "That," said the captain, "is the entrance to one of the most fertile valleys in the world. And you see the town on that triangular spit of land where the Shenandoah runs in from the south and the Potomac runs down from the west? That is Harpers Ferry, where we get off. She is in Union army hands now."

Zack nodded as he stared down at the town of Harpers Ferry. A Union flag flew over it, and Union cannons stood on the hills overlooking the town. Across the Potomac, seeming to rise straight out of the river, was a still larger mountain, and its peak, too, bristled with Union guns.

"Looks peaceful enough," drawled a tall dark-haired soldier leaning over to look from the window near the captain. "Been on leave myself." As he spoke he extended his hand to shake the captain's. The soldier had one of the largest hands Zack had ever seen. "Lieutenant Stone, here."

Captain Hale shook his hand. "Mark Hale, here, with orders to report to General Sullivan at Harpers Ferry. From what I've heard, Mosby's band of raiders have been keeping our men on their toes around here."

"You heard right there," Stone agreed. "There's hundreds of square miles of forested mountains in these parts, small towns, country lanes, farms, and wooded lots all full of southern folks ready to hide Mosby and his men. Officially, Mosby's men are the 43rd Battalion of Virginia Cavalry, better known as Mosby's Rangers. We hear he reports directly to General Robert E. Lee. Mosby has close to two thousand men. They strike anywhere, from the outskirts of Washington, across the Blue Ridge Mountains, into the Shenandoah Valley, and beyond the Potomac River into Maryland." Stone seated himself across from the captain.

In a lowered voice he confided, "Wouldn't want this to get to General Sullivan's ears, but Mosby is one name the men around here respect as much as they hate it. He strikes like lightning, and many a soldier has lost his life or his horse or both before he knew what was happening. You can bet on it, when our men go out on picket duty they're nervous as cats. Mosby's men ride at night or by day, in good or bad weather, where you expect them, and where you don't."

"It sounds like Mosby is one big thorn in the Union army's flank," Captain Hale said. Zack smiled to himself at the captain's description.

"The worst of it," Stone continued, "is that, false alarms or real, the men can't get a decent night's sleep with Mosby's men apt to show up anywhere anytime. Don't take more than a squirrel scurrying through dry leaves to set the men sounding the alarm." He chuckled softly. "Trouble is, with the real shortage of manpower in this army right now we can't hardly afford the infantry and cavalry to guard our supply wagon trains. Mosby seems to know where to hit."

Captain Hale nodded. "I expect he will be even more active as our troops take over the valley."

"You can count on that," Stone said. "I've a score to settle with one of his men myself." He rubbed the side of his nose. "Got this during one of Mosby's midnight raids two months ago." From the corner of his eye Zack noted a thin scar on the left side of Lieutenant Stone's nose.

With a lurch the train pulled to a stop at the station. Zack followed Captain Hale from the station up the steep slope into town. Union guns gleamed on the heights. It looked to Zack like that Mosby and his men wouldn't dare attack Harpers Ferry.

10

On the March

The captain's tent stood in a row with other officers' tents away from the enlisted men's. There were no black soldiers at this camp as far as Zack could see, though plenty of the workers not in uniform were Negroes. He thought he glimpsed a black boy hurrying into an officer's tent a few feet away. He wasn't surprised, since many officer's boys were blacks.

Quickly Zack went to work brushing away the dust of the journey. He laid out the items he knew must be polished before dress parade and put every article in its exact position army style. On the box that served as a table the captain had already set up a framed photo. Zack picked it up and studied the young woman and small boy in the picture. She had a sweet face, and the boy looked much like her. The sound of footsteps made Zack turn with the picture still in his hand.

Captain Hale stood quietly eyeing the tent and then Zack. Without a word he reached for the picture, held it for a moment, then set it down gently on the box. "Beautiful, aren't they?" he said. "That is my wife and son. When you look at that picture, Zack, you see the best part of me."

Zack smiled. "Yes, sir," he said.

With an answering smile the captain picked up his dress coat. "I have an invitation to dine with the colonel tonight. When you are through here I have nothing more to require of you for this evening."

Zack helped the captain into his uniform. When the captain had left he hurried to finish his work. He was eager to find the tent he would share with a colored cook from New Orleans.

The cook was a short wiry little man with frizzy gray hair and a thick southern accent. Zack strained to make out his words. "'Spect you keep everythin' shinin' and we got no trouble," he said with a sweep of his arm toward Zack's side of the tent. "Don't nobody go pokin' in my things and we do jus' fine." With a secretive smile on his face he held up a tin box and opened it to show Zack the small sacks within. A fragrant mixture of smells came from the sacks. "Brung them all the way from home. Can't get nothin' like these here herbs 'round this place. A pinch of this and that and some good ole pepper done make me the best cook in these parts. 'Spect I be gettin' a package from home one of these days. Got to keep my supply up."

Zack liked the old man from the start, and so long as the cook talked slowly enough he could catch most of what he said. Jeb was his name, and he was curious about how Zack had landed in the army.

At Zack's mention of New York City Jeb's eyes sparkled with interest. "Lot of folks 'round here talkin' about up north, and now I goin' to find out what you got to say. Tell me about colored folks livin' in grand houses just like white folk."

Zack shook his head. "Ain't seen that," Zack said. "Never saw that, but I did see Chaplain Turner at the grand meetin' last January to celebrate President Lincoln's Emancipation Proclamation to free the slaves. Now that was a meetin' New York City won't forget." As Jeb listened, Zack described the men who had come from everywhere to give speeches and how at the end the mighty throng of people had lifted their voices to sing "The Battle Hymn of the Republic."

"Ain't that somethin' now," Jeb said. "You got to tell that to the others when we has our time 'round the campfire."

Outside the tent a loud cry rose that brought Jeb to his feet instantly. "Mosby's men attacked the camp at Duffield. They're bringing the wounded in now." Duffield was only a few miles outside of Harpers Ferry. Jeb ran from the tent, and Zack followed him. Men were hurrying from everywhere toward the entrance to the camp. Two long lines of soldiers formed on either side of the entry road as wagons bearing the wounded and dead rolled past. A line of infantrymen, the soldiers who fought on foot, followed. Some of them limped along, others were supported by their friends.

"Made off with most of the mules and supplies," an infantry soldier called out. "Waited till the cavalry left before they surprised us." The cavalry were soldiers who fought on horseback.

Another man added, "Wouldn't any of us be here now if the cavalry hadn't come back after they heard the shooting. Would have won, too, if Mosby hadn't hidden some of his men in the pines on Peter's Bluff. Soon as the patrol came back them raiders rushed out and attacked. The other half of Mosby's men took off with the stuff and some of our men as prisoners. Didn't bother with us wounded," he said and hobbled on to join his fellows.

"Them raiders is mean as warthogs. If they can't exchange them poor prisoners for something they want, they just go and hang 'em. Never know when you gonna meet up with that Mosby." Jeb shook his head. "Ain't nobody safe, with them mountains all around the valley out there," he warned.

In the weeks that followed, Zack had forgotten Jeb's warning. This morning it wasn't danger but excitement that filled his mind. The army was on the move. The long line of march stretched out for fourteen miles. Seated on the cook's wagon beside Jeb, it looked to Zack like an unbroken line of white canvased wagons as far ahead as he could see. They. had left camp at four A.M. two days ago, crossed the Opequon Creek at Berryville, and taken the Berryville Pike to Valley Pike, a road that cut through the length of the valley. Somewhere up ahead, Captain Hale rode with the cavalry guards ahead of the supply wagons. The captain had made it clear that Zack's place was with Jeb in the supply wagon while the army was in the field. But from where Zack sat it was all one long army line, and he was a part of it.

The wagons moved easily on the stone-paved road. All through the valley they had passed farms lush with early growth and small towns with neat red-brick and gray-limestone houses. The Blue Ridge Mountains on the east were alive with spring blooms. How could anyone imagine a war going on in such a place?

Zack was beginning to feel hungry when the startling sound of drums boomed across the valley like a long roll of thunder. The sound, unlike anything Zack had heard before, reached his very insides.

Jeb pulled on the horses to hold them steady. "That means action, boy. They calls it the long roll, and don't never hear it 'cept when they is a battle comin'." As Jeb pulled the wagon to a stop, word came down the line shouted from wagon to wagon, "Rebels ahead at New Market." Zack felt his stomach sink. This was it, a real battle with the Confederate soldiers known to the Union men as rebels or rebs.

"Hold them lines," Jeb ordered, "while I see what's goin' on." As Jeb scrambled from the wagon the sound of distant artillery fire made the horses move nervously.

"Easy now," Zack soothed. "I don't like what I'm hearin' any more than you do." The sound of the big guns firing grew louder by the minute.

11

Battle at New Market

T hem guns mean business," Jeb shouted as he climbed back into the wagon and took the reins. Zack held tightly to the wagon seat while Jeb urged the horses on. Infantry guards hurried past on either side of the wagons.

"Ain't no room here," Jeb yelled above the noise. "The Shenandoah River be runnin' along here on one side of us and Swift's Creek's on our other side. Can't nobody cross that creek or that river. Rain done swoll 'em up too high. Only one way to go and that be straight on." The battle to take New Market would have to be fought on the narrow ground between the flooded waters.

Zack nodded. The valley seemed to be alive with the deep boom of artillery fire. The closer they came to the town the more deafening the noise grew. A soldier on horseback ordered Jeb to pull up his wagon behind one of the low hills where a hospital tent was set up to tend the wounded.

"You two," the surgeon commanded, "over here." Zack was sent to fetch water while Jeb kindled a fire to heat it. On a hill above the town of New Market the enemy troops' big guns roared. On this side the Union guns thundered from the crest of the nearby hill. The earth seemed to shake under Zack's feet as he ran to fill his pails of water from a small stream.

The battle had hardly begun and already wounded men were stumbling toward the hospital. As the numbers of wounded grew, fear gripped Zack. His stomach lurched at the sight of a soldier's dangling arm, and he turned and ran behind the cook's wagon. He was going to be sick. Only he wasn't alone.

A few feet away Jeb crooned to a young white soldier lying on the ground with his head in Jeb's lap. "You gonna be all right soon. Just you think 'bout how glad your mama gonna be when this war is over. That's it, you rest now." Zack turned away. The young man's blood already soaked the ground under him.

"You okay, boy?" It was Jeb. His hand on Zack's shoulder squeezed lightly. "Ain't no more I can do for that soldier," he said. "The way these fellows is pourin' in here, the surgeon can't keep up with 'em. Most of these poor fellows give anythin' for a drink of water. You reckon you can see they gets some?" he asked.

Zack stood up and brushed the dirt from his pants. "I reckon," he said. As Jeb left to tend another soldier, Zack went back to where the wounded waited, some sitting on the ground, others lying where their companions had laid them. He brought water and dipped it out for the men until it was gone and then fetched more. He lost track of how many times he refilled the water buckets. The groans and weeping of the badly wounded made him want to turn away, but he gritted his teeth and held the dipper of water for those who couldn't hold it.

It seemed to Zack that he could hear a new sound, the popping of rifles much nearer now than before. The wounded continued to come. Overhead the sky darkened then burst into a downpour. Zack did his best to cover some of the men lying in the mud with rubber blankets. His feet sunk in the churned-up mud that was fast becoming thick. Some of the men had lost their shoes in it. One of the great guns sounded nearby, and a soldier lying on the ground screamed. Zack shivered. Nothing seemed to stop the battle, not even the storm overhead.

At the edge of the field, to the right of the foot of the hill where the hospital had been set up, a figure stumbled then fell. No one stopped to help him as other wounded staggered past toward the hospital. His feet slogging in the heavy mud Zack ran to the field and knelt by the soldier. The pale face of a young man looked at him with pleading eyes. "Help me, please," he begged. "I been hit in the stomach."

Zack took off his jacket and laid it under the soldier's head. "I'll get help," he promised. "It's gonna be all right."

He stood up to go, only it was already too late. The soldier's mouth lay open and his eyes stared unseeing. Gently Zack took his jacket and ran blindly toward the hospital tent.

In the heavy rain the ground beneath the horse's hooves was a sea of mud. Captain Hale reined in his horse. The enemy were directly ahead across a cornfield and behind a low hill. "Steady," he coaxed the horse who moved restlessly under him. "All in good time, old girl," he said. With a look at the cavalry behind him awaiting his signal, the captain raised his arm. "Charge!" he cried. In a thunder of hooves the men urged their horses across the field. Green stalks of new corn flattened beneath their feet as they galloped. Cannons roared. Captain Hale felt the blood pounding in his ears. Bullets flew past him as he led his men forward, and then the rebels came like a gray wave rushing toward them.

The captain swerved his horse to the right where the line looked thinner. They could break through there and get behind the enemy's cannons. "Follow me," he shouted into the pounding rain and the thunder of the big guns. Left and right men were going down under the steady enemy fire. The captain leaned low on his horse's back. "Come on, girl. We've got to take out those guns." Suddenly his horse reared and fell, wounded in the chest. The captain scrambled to his feet and ran on toward the hill.

From the hilltop the long high-pitched rebel yell rent the air as troops of gray-uniformed soldiers with fixed bayonets came swarming down the hill. Stunned, the captain saw that the enemy soldiers before him were boys, young cadets not yet out of military school. He gasped in horror as they came on, screaming their battle cry. His hands froze on the handle of his gun. A second later a bullet tore into his stomach, and then another as he fell.

Behind the Union lines the wounded continued to stream toward the hospital. Zack heard a soldier whose left arm hung limp at his side report to the doctor that the rebels had thrown a bunch of teenage cadets into the battle. "Them boys was acting crazy, hollering and running straight into our guns. Never seen anything like it. Don't know how they did it, but they took the hill away from our men before we could could stop 'em." The battle was not going well. By early afternoon the order came to retreat.

Ambulance wagons were loaded, but there were too few for the number of wounded. Some were put into other wagons, including Jeb's cook wagon, for transport back to Harpers Ferry. They were about to leave when a fresh wave of wounded arrived. Among the soldiers carried in was a figure Zack recognized. With a cry he leaped from the wagon and ran. The man on the litter was Captain Hale!

The doctor knelt by the captain to examine the gaping wounds in his stomach and chest. "I'm afraid it won't be long, Captain," the doctor said. Kneeling on the other side of the captain, Zack gasped.

Captain Hale looked up at him and whispered, "Zack, stay, please." The doctor nodded at Zack as he stood. "Let the boy stay. He can ride with me later and help with the wounded." Jeb's was the last wagon besides the doctor's to leave, but Zack didn't see it go.

He bent his head above Captain Hale's. "You hurtin' bad, I know," he said, "but you just hold on, sir, for your boy's sake and his mama's." Tears filled his eyes, and gently he took the officer's cold hand in his.

"Zack, I'm going. Remember you said God is the one friend we can't do without? Tell my wife I'll be waiting for her and little Luke. Heaven. . . ." His voice faded, and his eyes closed.

Zack pressed the captain's hand to his chest. "I'll tell her, don't you worry none. Jesus is gonna take you home, and they'll be comin', too, one day." Tears streamed down his face. There was no Chaplain Turner with words of comfort. In a choked voice Zack said the words he knew best. "The Lord is my shepherd. Though I walk through the valley of death I will fear no evil." Captain Hale lay still and silent. His hand in Zack's was limp, and Zack knew he was gone. Later someone loosened Zack's hands from the captain's hand still clutched against his chest. In the hospital wagon filled with wounded Zack huddled in a corner. The retreat of the Union soldiers back down the valley was complete, and for many their last battle was finally over.

At Strasburg, twenty miles from the battle at New Market, the army rested, and Zack made his way to Jeb's tent. Jeb looked up from the small campfire he had been tending. "Thought you would be comin' 'bout now," he said gently. "Got some coffee here if you wants some."

"No thanks," Zack answered. "Guess I'll turn in for the night." Jeb nodded, and Zack slipped into the tent and threw himself onto its dirt floor. He was too tired to think anymore. During the night someone covered him with a blanket as he slept.

It was a sorry looking army that made its way back to Harpers Ferry. When they reached camp Zack slipped away.

He had to make one final visit to the captain's tent. On the box that served as a table lay the last letter from Mrs. Hale. Zack picked up her picture, stared at it, then put it down gently. He had to give her the captain's message. His arms felt heavy and his eyes wanted to close, but somehow he managed to write. Finished at last, he slipped the letter into his pocket and went to look for Jeb.

12

Mule Sense

Zack rubbed his sore shoulders. His muscles ached from the past weeks of hauling boxes for the quartermaster, loading and unloading supplies. No more shipments were expected this morning, but Jeb was sure to need him to fetch water.

At the cookhouse Jeb handed him the water bucket. "You just in time," he said. As Zack returned with the water Jeb met him. "Let's go," he said. "The mail done come, and I got a feelin' in my bones my package be there. Maybe today you gonna hear from your young friend," he added.

"You mean Caleb? I reckon it could be any day now." Zack steeled himself for another disappointment as he listened for his name. Maybe Caleb had not received the letter Zack had written him.

"Zack Boone, where are you, man?"

"Here," Zack shouted as he made his way through the group of men waiting for mail. With the long-awaited letter in hand he hurried to his tent to read it.

Dear Zack,

You ask about Chaplin Turner and I fownd out he
is a lot beter Sargint Trask says. Trask says he don
spect him back til the end of sumer. He says Company B mite be movin out to Petersberg wher the
battel is. I wil rite you ther. My new dril sargint is
yung and he is gud to the men. He is from New
Hampsha a northen state. Moses has got movd up
to corprl and the men is mity glad. I am techin
drum to a new boy frum Kintucky. He is a gud
lerner same as you. Rite soon.

Your frend, Caleb

Zack sat quietly with his knees drawn up. It was
too soon to hope that the chaplain was back. With
Captain Hale gone there was nothing to keep him
here now. As soon as Chaplain Turner got well he
would write to him and ask him for a transfer back
as his assistant. Meanwhile, he would just have to
wait.

He had almost forgotten about his letter to the
captain's wife when the following week an answer
came. He read the letter slowly, then reread the
final words: "I can never thank you enough for writing to me. I shall be praying for your safety and the
end of this terrible war which has cost us all so
dearly. Your friend, Mrs. G. Hale."

Next he read again his letter from Ben's cousin
Abigail. Zack smiled broadly at her words. "I hope
you like the cookies I sent. I made up the recipe

myself." The cookies had not come yet, but Zack could imagine Abigail doing battle with the cookie dough until it looked right to her.

That night he dreamed he was sent home from the army back to New York City. In his dream Ben and his family became a marching band who met him as he descended the ramp of a large steamboat. Abigail, with her red hair flying loose in the wind, held up a giant plate of cookies to him. The sound of Jeb moving about the tent woke him.

"Time you be up, boy," Jeb said. "You remember what I tole you now 'bout not takin' no sass from them mules. Seein' how you feel 'bout horses I tole the sergint you was his boy for this here job. I 'spect you gonna prove me true, boy."

Zack stood up quickly. This was the day he started his new duty with the wagon drivers. Only instead of horses he would be learning to work with mules. "A mule can't be a powerful lot different from a horse," Zack said. "Nothin' to fret about, Jeb."

A boy who looked to be no more than fifteen stood leaning lazily against a tree next to where the mules were quartered. The boy kept his eyes on Zack's face. He didn't look away as Zack approached, nor did Zack.

Zack was first to speak. "Sergeant Lewis said to ask for someone named Shawn. I reckon that might be you."

A slow smile spread across the boy's face. "I'm supposin' he told you to look for a tall skinny kid with freckles on his face?"

Now it was Zack's turn to grin. That was exactly what Sergeant Lewis had said, only he had added "brown hair with a cowlick."

"So, it's yourself must be the new man I'm to be showing how to drive old Molly and Peg. Then let's be gettin' on with it." Zack reached out a hand to stroke the reddish-brown mule named Molly. Her great dark eyes watched his every movement. Her long ears twitched, and quick as lightning the mule nicked his hand with her strong teeth. Zack jumped back. "Whoa, there. That ain't no way to greet a fellow," he said rubbing his stinging hand.

"Could have told you Molly don't take to strangers," Shawn said. "First thing you got to do is make friends."

Zack nodded. Couldn't Shawn see that's what he had been doing? Any horse would have known. Mules must be pretty dumb or else plain ornery.

"Talking won't do you no good till she gets to know you," Shawn went on. "Ought to let you find out for yourself." He patted the mule's side. Molly shivered but stood patiently while Shawn rubbed her down. "Better start with a lump of sugar," he said to Zack. "Like your sweets, don't you, old girl?"

Gingerly Zack took the sugar Shawn handed him and held it out. Molly acted wary but finally let him feed her. As soon as the sugar was gone she bit

Zack again. "You cut that out," he hollered and slapped her smartly on her flank. With her lips drawn back Molly gave what looked like a wicked grin.

Shawn shook his finger at the mule. "Molly, me girl, you mind your manners. Now, me lad," he said to Zack, "you'll be needing to watch your step with the lass here until she's after making up her mind about you."

For the rest of the day Zack worked with Shawn and the mules. Whenever he got too close to Molly she nipped him and once or twice nearly kicked him. The other mule, Peg, didn't seem to care who fed her, but she might as well have been deaf when Zack gave an order to move or turn. Several times Zack caught Shawn grinning as if he enjoyed the spectacle of Zack's frustration with the two stubborn mules.

Tired and angry at the end of the day Zack was glad to flop onto his pallet. "Can't be anything worse than a mule," he said to Jeb, who was studying a worn spelling book.

Jeb looked up with a sly smile. "Yes, sah, I reckon that's right lessen it be a mule driver what smells so bad I can't hardly keep my mind on this here book."

Zack sat up instantly and held his hands up to sniff them. It was true. The strong odor of the mules had stuck to him. How could he not have noticed it? There was just time, if he hurried, to make it to the creek for a wash. The water was cold, but Zack

didn't care. He shivered and scrubbed first himself
then his clothes. Dressed in his sopping uniform
pants and shirt he ran back to the tent.

"You crazy, boy?" Jeb demanded. "You know the
army don'low no laundry 'cept on Mondays. Where
you reckon you gonna dry them things?" Grum-
bling all the while, Jeb rose and stood over Zack.
"You get them wet things off you, boy. Old Jeb is
gonna take 'em back to the cookin' fire away from
pryin' eyes. Can't taken 'em to the campfire less
somebody shootin' off his mouth 'bout doin' laundry. I 'spect nobody gonna trouble me for heatin'
up some coffee for officers what might be wantin'
some. Guess I can lay them clothes close enuff so
as they dry out."

Zack had forgotten that army rules not only said
when a fellow could do laundry but exactly where
and how high the lines had to be to hang it for drying. "I'm obliged to you, Jeb," he said. As Jeb left
with the clothes Zack groaned aloud. Whatever he
wore to work, whether it smelled of mules or not,
there would be no doing laundry except on Mondays. He couldn't ask Jeb to risk drying his things
again.

When Jeb returned with the dry clothes tattoo
was just sounding. "No more time for studyin',"
Jeb complained. "Just one thing, boy, I got to say.
Gonna be lots of times folks be teasin' you. I 'spect
sometimes even say you smell like a mule." Zack
thought he heard Jeb chuckle in the dark. "Now
don't you be rushin' off doin' the first thing comes

into your head like tonight, jumpin' in the creek 'fore a body could say hold on a minute. You got to learn when a body's needin' to laugh at hisself. Don' hurt to go 'long with a joke when the Lord knows it's true enough. Ain't like the good Lord done take away all the soap and water in this world so as you won't never have no bath agin. Just you be glad he done made you a man and not a mule."

Zack smiled at Jeb's last words and then laughed. In the dark Jeb laughed, and the two of them roared. Finally, gasping for breath and holding his aching sides, Zack stopped. "'Night," he whispered, "and thanks, Jeb."

All day Shawn had been laughing at him. For all he knew, that mule was laughing at him too. He thought of Chaplain Turner's horse Shadow. Anybody could be proud of a horse like that, but who cared about a dumb long-eared mule?

13

Fire in the Valley

Molly had learned to expect her daily treat of sugar from Zack, but this morning Zack was too slow giving it to her. Before he could lift his hand from his pocket she nipped him hard. Shawn, who had seen the whole thing, chuckled. Zack whirled about to face him, and then he laughed. "Got to be quicker than a mule 'round here," he said.

"That's the spirit!" Shawn cried. "Some folks just don't appreciate a smart mule. Now me, I know better. A good mule won't panic out in the field like a horse will. They can outrun a horse, too, and outlast them in the heat. Mules are smaller than horses but a whole lot smarter." Lifting one of Molly's hooves to inspect it he said, "Never you mind, my girl. It's small feet you're having, but no horse can outlast you." He put Molly's foot down gently and looked up at Zack. "My pa was the best mule team driver in this army before the fever took him." Shawn patted Molly's head. "Soon as this war is over it's a farm I'll be after and a pair of the finest mules I can find. A fellow has to be keeping hold of his dreams. I'm supposing you've got a dream of your own?"

After a minute's silence Zack answered. "I reckon I want to be a teacher more than anything. Never thought I'd say so, but since I been in the army I kind of got to like teachin' some of the men to read."

"Never, now. You don't mean to be telling me you can read?" Shawn's voice grew soft. "Pa and me didn't stay long enough in one place so as I could get me schooling."

An idea flashed before Zack. "I'll make you a bargain," he said. "You learn me all there is to know about mules, and I'll sure teach you how to read."

"Done," Shawn said.

Zack borrowed Jeb's primer and began lessons the next day. Shawn puzzled over the letters at first, and then all at once his eyes lit up. "*B* sounds like a lamb calling for his ma when you put it with *a*. Fix on *d* you got *bad*. With a wide smile he looked at Zack. "This learning ain't so bad, after all." Zack laughed. For his part, Shawn had shown him how to handle the lines that guided teams of four and six mules at once. It might come in handy, even though for now he was assigned two mules and a lighter wagon load.

The summer rains left behind them the smell of fresh fields growing and wild flowers blooming on the nearby hills. "A body could get a hankering to farm in this place," Shawn remarked as he fed grain to the mules.

Watching a flight of birds overhead, Zack agreed. "It sure looks peaceful. But I'm thinkin' how it really ain't." Only yesterday more wounded had come in to report another raid by Mosby's men on a Union patrol. "Between Mosby's attacks and rebel troops popping in and out of the mountain passes to fight and run, it's peaceful like a mountain lion sunning himself."

Tensions in camp mounted. The men were to be evacuated to a safe distance. Zack rode out beside Shawn to the new camp. All down the line the news was that the Southern leader Jubal Early had attacked Washington, D.C., and might sweep this way. The July heat felt like a hot furnace as the small Union force left. Sweat ran down Zack's back under his woolen shirt. "You reckon the Confederates will take the capital?" he asked.

"If they do," Shawn replied, "we will be seeing a lot more Union troops fighting in this valley." The Shenandoah Valley was a wide corridor that led right to the back door into Washington, D.C., and on to the north. The mountains bordering the valley made it easier for rebel troops to swoop in from the mountain passes to attack the North. They also made it easier for the enemy to hide when Union troops appeared.

A week later Shawn came running with a newspaper in his hand. "The capital is safe, and the rebels are on the run. It says here they burned a town in Pennsylvania but never got inside Washington, D.C." Zack felt a great weight roll off his shoulders. The war was still raging, but the capital was saved.

Back in camp at Harpers Ferry Zack brushed his uniform and polished his boots. A new commander was coming to the Shenandoah Valley. "Now we gonna see action," Jeb stated. "Ginral Grant just be done foolin' with them Mosby raiders and them rebel soldjas. You watch, boy, 'cause things is heatin' up 'round here."

Zack and Shawn stood with the drivers as the troops welcomed the new general. Zack could see why the men called him "Little Phil" Sheridan. The general was a short man with a large head and extremely long arms which might have caused laughter had his black eyes not been so piercing even from a distance. There was an air of authority about him in spite of his height.

"My orders are to clean out this valley so that a crow flying over it will have to bring his own provisions," the general cried out in a booming voice. The men responded with cheers.

Shawn's voice was bursting with pride. "The general's an Irishman, and you can bet on some real fighting now." Zack was quiet. The memory of Captain Hale's death at the battle of New Market came back to his mind. He never wanted to see another battle like New Market.

Six days later the first wagon train of supplies followed the general and his troops from Harpers Ferry toward Cedar Creek.

Shawn and Zack were not among those ordered to be on this first supply train. A day later, riders brought word that Mosby's raiders had attacked and destroyed wagons, captured prisoners, and carried off horses, mules, and beef cattle. Zack glanced at the look of anger on Shawn's face. Not even his beloved Irish general was beyond losing wagons to the likes of Mosby. It was a blow to Shawn's pride.

No army could move without its lifeline of supplies. Three wagon trains a week moved out of Harpers Ferry to the front where General Sheridan and his troops were. Shawn and Zack were busy now. Zack had never seen such long lines. Usually five hundred wagons made up a train, but now and then they numbered one thousand. As Shawn drove he explained what Zack needed to watch for. "If you have a thousand wagons to move, the line has got to be ten miles long. That means when the lead wagon passes a certain point it will take four hours until the last wagon reaches that same place. The farther the general goes the longer the line stretches back to the supply stations. You get the picture?" he asked.

"I reckon that's a lot of line to guard," Zack replied. "Seems like we got more infantry escort guarding the wagons than up fightin' with the general." The wagons carried rations, ammunition, and clothing necessary for the troops. The fearsome Mosby Rangers might attack anywhere along the line, steal the provisions and livestock, and be off before the lead wagon drivers knew what happened.

One morning Zack awoke shaking with chills and fever. Jeb hovered over him like a mother hen. For days Zack lay sick. When the fever left, his legs felt weak and wobbly as a newborn calf's. "'Bout time we get some meat back on them bones," Jeb said. "This soup never fail me yet," he insisted when Zack puckered his lips at the thick, greasy taste.

While the fever ran through the camp striking many of the men, another battle raged. General Sheridan and the rest of the army fought the rebels at the town of Winchester and won. The Battle of Fisher's Hill followed, and again the Union won. Zack was fully recovered now and glad to be free of Jeb's special herb teas and strengthening soup.

Late in October the Union soldiers crumpled before a fierce, unexpected attack by Southern forces at a place in the valley called Cedar Creek. Shawn and Zack's wagon became an ambulance for the wounded in retreat with the rest of the army. Their wagon was well away from the battle front when the news came that the general had saved the day. Shawn cheered till he was hoarse. "Did you hear it, Zack? The general himself came galloping across the fields on his black stallion calling the men to follow him back to the battle. Aye, that is a man for you." Shawn's faith in his Irish general had returned. Zack breathed a sigh of relief. At least there would be no rebel soldiers following after them.

This morning as Zack headed toward the stables he noticed a strange smell in the air. Standing outside the wooden stable door Shawn motioned for him to hurry, and Zack quickened his pace. He could see other drivers running to the hill on the south of the camp.

"The whole valley is burning!" Shawn cried. "You can smell it and see the smoke from the top of the hill." Together they raced to the hilltop. It was true. To the south a huge dark cloud rose in the sky and stretched as far as they could see. The smell of fire wafted toward him and made Zack's eyes burn.

Ahead of him the familiar figure of Jeb moved away from the group of men staring up the valley. Jeb shook his head. "Terrible thing to see," he said. "Won't be no more food comin' out of this valley to feed them rebs. I just hates to see the Lord's good crops goin' up in smoke. Lucky for me, my time in this here army be up next week, and I am goin' as far north as a fellow can go."

"I fear 'tis a lot of folks won't be eating come this winter," Shawn said. "It's orders, and the general has to carry them out. The troops will be burning every barn and mill and crop in the valley."

A driver standing nearby pointed to the hills in the distance. "Them's soldiers posted on the crests of them hills. Won't be any farmers hiding their stock on the mountainsides. The livestock, everythin' is government property now," he said. "Yup, it belongs to the government down to the last chicken."

Shawn's voice grew soft. "I wouldna' want to be living down there." Zack stared in disbelief at the darkening valley.

14
Raiders

As the day wore on, wagons of refugees from the destroyed valley farms streamed into camp. Some of the refugees wore the clothes of Mennonites, a religious group of people who did not believe in fighting. They had refused to fight for the South, even though they lived in the Virginia valley. Their farms, too, had been burned along with others. A young mother with a pale face held her new baby close, while two small children clung to her skirts. From his pocket Zack took a handful of candies and offered them to the boys. The woman began to weep, and Zack lowered his eyes. With nothing left to live on but the few possessions piled in their wagons, the refugees were seeking passes to go north.

The beautiful valley Zack had seen when he first came with the captain was now a blackened wasteland. Only the bare houses were spared. But even these were burned when their owners were suspected of helping the rebels. An evil peace had come to the valley. Zack could feel the loneliness of the valley's ruins as ash-covered wagons, smelling of smoke, continued to roll into camp. Tonight he would write Chaplain Turner at the camp in Petersburg. From Caleb's last letter he guessed the chaplain should have caught up with Company B by now.

"What you writin'?" Jeb asked.

Zack felt his face grow hot. "Just writin' a letter to Chaplain Turner down in Petersburg." The truth that he had asked the chaplain to get him transferred back to Company B stuck in his throat. "I got to let him know about Captain Hale. Guess you know how the army is. Might be I'll have to go back if the chaplain is needin' me."

Jeb went on sorting his new packets of spices. "I hear the fightin' at Petersburg done took a lot of good men out of this world already, and ain't no end in sight yet. 'Course, if that be where you got to go, then you just got to go."

Zack bit his lip. He didn't want to see any more fighting, but neither did he want to stay here in the valley. Anyway, it would be different helping Chaplain Turner. Like Moses once said, the Lord was on the chaplain's side. Zack bent his head and went on writing.

At the end of the week Jeb left the army. "I'll miss you, boy," he'd said. Though the lump in his throat felt huge as he waved back at Jeb, Zack managed to say, "I'll miss you too."

Zack had little time to mope. The army now had large numbers of animals taken away from the valley farmers. A new team of mules had come under Shawn's care. They were beauties, sleek and young. Shawn's eyes sparkled. "Will you look at them!"

he said. "It's time you took over old Molly and Peg. I'll be seein' to these two myself. Well, lad, go on now. They're all yours." Shawn had a gleam in his eye as Zack looked doubtfully at the two older mules.

Zack gritted his teeth and went to work. Molly no longer eyed him as her personal enemy, but both mules were still stubbornly true to their nature and obeyed only when they pleased. The rest of the time, Zack coaxed and even tricked them into obeying. Abigail's cookies, hard as rocks when they arrived in camp, worked well as a bribe. Zack was sorry to see the last of them go. Each short run with the wagon became a contest between Zack and the mules. Shawn shook his head as he watched.

On longer drives Shawn drove his new team, and Zack sat beside him on the wagon. Molly and Peg remained at camp. "Got to break these new fellows in," Shawn explained. "Might need your help," he added. Zack knew that was not the real reason Shawn had not let him take a wagon on his own. A single wagon out of line could slow up the rest. In a retreat or under fire the road had to be clear for men and artillery to move past the wagons. Zack just could not count on Molly and Peg to obey him yet.

By mid-November General Sheridan's main army withdrew from the valley to help General Grant's armies at Petersburg, where the fighting was heaviest. The supply lines still had to be maintained, and Zack and Shawn kept busy. Though the valley was in Union hands, skirmishes, fights too small to be called battles, still went on between bands of rebels and the Union troops left in the valley. But the biggest problem was Mosby and his men, who continued to raid Union outposts and wagon trains and carry off prisoners. There was a constant need for new wagon drivers.

"Think you can handle a wagon of your own?" Shawn asked.

Zack had just finished feeding Molly and Peg. The cool November air made the mules frisky, and Zack patted Molly's neck.

"Reckon I can handle these two one way or another," Zack replied. "Suppose I'll be drawin' driver's pay too?" He smiled broadly at Shawn.

"Now, how could I be telling you that when the army is already two months late with our pay?" Shawn retorted. "Just don't you be landing me in the guardhouse by losing your wagon or tangling up the line." Shawn grinned and pummeled Zack's shoulder. "You'll do fine, me lad," he said in his best Irish.

When the day came to form the next wagon train, Zack's wagon, hitched to Molly and Peg, was close to the end of the line. Shawn's was too far ahead in the lead for Zack to see. "It's okay," Zack soothed Molly. "You and Peg don't have nothin' to worry 'bout. It's me that's got to do the worryin'."

The day was warm for November. Zack's woolen shirt felt hot, and he had laid his jacket beside him on the wagon seat. By the time the wagons ahead had begun to pass near one of the gaps in the Blue Ridge Mountains it was late afternoon. Shadows darkened the trees. Zack flicked the reins to bring Molly and Peg closer to the wagon in front of them. As the wagon jerked, a thundering noise sounded behind him. Out of nowhere a band of riders raced toward the wagon train.

It was impossible to turn the wagons without running into those ahead or behind. Zack tried to hold Molly and Peg as the mules reared. The driver ahead of him moved sideways. In moments the road became a tangled mass of wagons swerving out of line. Rebel yells and gunshots filled the air. Zack couldn't think what to do, and then Molly decided for him. He tried to hold her, but the mule pulled to the right straight toward the trees by the side of the road. The wagon missed a large tree by a few inches as they went crashing through the underbrush and out onto a dirt road. It was one of the many mountain paths that led off the main road.

With all his might Zack pulled on the reins, but the mules were spooked. They ran like the wind, pulling the wagon and Zack along. Shots and cries sounded close behind him. Zack looked back, but what he saw was little comfort. Horsemen driving stolen mules and cattle before them were coming down the road toward him. Zack braced his knees against the wagon and leaned out over the mules. "Faster, faster," he urged. The road wound suddenly in a dizzying spiral. Behind him the raiders, slowed by their plunder, came on steadily. If only he could get far enough ahead of them maybe he would have a chance. Where was the cavalry to catch the raiders? The road ahead continued twisting closer and closer now to the edge of a deep ravine. He didn't dare slow the mules even if he could. But at this speed the wagon was dangerously near the steep mountain edge. He wasn't sure if he closed his eyes as he prayed, "Lord, help me." Zack didn't see the rider in the flashing gray uniform and turned-up hat of the Mosby Rangers who galloped up beside him. With a crack the man's rifle butt struck the side of Zack's head. A blaze of lights tore through Zack's head, and then he knew no more.

The force of the blow had knocked Zack's body from the wagon as it passed close to the ravine. He fell to the ground and rolled over the edge. The wagon still plunged ahead until the man was able to grab the reins. Behind him others raced to help. Within a short time the raiders were out of sight, and silence closed in on the mountain road.

At the edge of the ravine Zack's Union army cap lay in the dust. Like all army clothing it bore the number of its owner. Moments later gunshots rang out. A small party of stragglers from the raiders' band galloped down the road. Behind them rode the Union cavalry in full chase. Not two feet from Zack's hat a raider's horse was fatally wounded, fell to the ground, and threw its rider. The raider lay still as a second shot struck him. Two Union soldiers stopped to dismount by the body.

One of them peered at the dead raider. "It's one of Mosby's men all right, but it ain't Mosby." The soldier sounded disappointed.

Meanwhile, the man with him fished up Zack's cap on the end of his bayonet. "Afraid they got one of our boys. Better take this back to camp for identification," he said. Gingerly he glanced over the edge of the ravine. "Must have sent the body down there," he muttered. Shadows deepened around them as evening closed over the mountain road. The rest of the cavalry had galloped ahead of the two. "Let's get out of here," the soldier said as he stuffed Zack's cap inside his shirt. "Ain't nothing more here."

On a small outcrop of rock no more than six feet below the edge of the ravine Zack's body lay tangled in a mass of broken branches and leaves. His right leg was twisted under him and pressed hard against a thick branch. Blood seeped from a deep cut where the wood pressed against it. In the dark his eyelids fluttered, opened, then closed again.

15
Lost

Zack opened his eyes. The bed under him poked him in a dozen places, and he seemed to be lying in a strange cramped position. For some reason there were branches and leaves all around him. As he tried to move, a buzzing sound filled his ears. He stared up at the sky above him. It looked strange, like a small blue patch that kept shifting its shape as he watched. For a long time he lay still and let the warmth of the sun seep into his body.

Little by little he took in his surroundings. The steep smooth wall of stone above him came into focus. Slowly he pulled himself to a sitting position to look around. Somehow he had landed in a large bush or tree with his head inches away from its thick center trunk. He must have fallen onto it. He did not remember doing that. As the truth of the deep ravine below him and the sheer cliff above him became real he gripped the branches close to him. All that lay between him and the ravine was this ledge and the stunted trees that grew from it. Slowly, supporting his back against the thickest part of the tree, he sat up.

Something was running down his leg. The warm wetness seeped into his boot. The wetness puzzled him, and he brushed at it. It felt sticky and clung to his hand. He stared at the red stuff on his fingers: blood. He must have cut himself, but how had he done that?

At first he couldn't understand why his brown-skinned leg had turned white under the blood welling up below his knee. His stomach lurched as he understood. Bone. The bone was showing through the gash.

Without thinking, Zack tore the shirt from his chest and gasped as the pain in his head stabbed into his eyes. With shaking hands he wadded the shirt onto the wound. For a minute he wondered why he didn't feel it. Blood was already soaking through the cloth. The laces on his boot turned red. It seemed a long time before he finished undoing and redoing both bootlaces around his bandaged leg. Wearily he leaned his buzzing head against the tree branches. It was funny that he should be sitting here. He would rest a while, close his eyes, and maybe then he would go on. He wasn't sure where he was supposed to be going or why he was here. If he could just sleep it would be better. As the day wore on, clouds gathered, and a sudden rainstorm broke above the mountain. Water ran down his face and he closed his eyes. Once during the night he opened his eyes, closed them again, and buried his face deeper into the leaves away from the rain. When he woke with a start it was still raining.

There was something he had to do. Pain stabbed through his leg as he tried to move. It felt like a thousand bee stings. His ears buzzed, and when he moved his head too sharply it hurt. Zack rubbed his face with his hand. He'd better get going or the chaplain would be mad. A fallen branch lay near him, and he reached for it to pull it toward him. It was thick enough to lean on, its y-branched top forming a rest for his arm. He managed to stand by holding to the stick with one hand and the tree with the other. Bees buzzed around his head.

Minnesota, that was it. He had to get to Minnesota and find Ben. There was only one way to go and that was down. The ledge angled to the right behind the bush where it sloped toward a smaller ledge below. The walls of stone that formed the sides of the ravine were uneven. Some of the rocks jutted out, and others sported small bushes whose hardy roots had grown in cracks in the rock. From above, the descent looked impossibly steep. On closer look Zack thought he could manage with his stick to help. What was it he had to do? Whatever it was it would have to wait until he got down. Pain shot through his leg like a sharp sword slicing into him each time he put his weight on it. Partway down he lost his stick. His hands were raw and bloody from scraping against rocks and sharp branches. Desperately he made his way from stone outcrop to outcrop, bush to bush clinging, slipping, clutching, and sometimes sliding downward. Somehow the bushes held, and what seemed impossible happened. He was at the bottom. A shallow stream of water flowed between the stone walls. He lay next to it and drank his fill. For a long time he lay shivering with cold. Above him the walls of the mountainside towered.

He had to get up. There was something he needed to do, only he had forgotten what. Pain shot through his leg and forced him back. After a while he saw what he needed. Broken tree limbs, stout enough for canes, lay close by the stream. With the top branches stripped away they would do. He pulled himself toward the sticks. Using two sticks to help him Zack stumbled to his feet. His leg hurt and his head pounded. He would have to go slowly.

It was hard walking along the ravine bottom. Stones and sticks were everywhere. At the far end of the ravine he found a gap that led out into a thick woods. The woods seemed deserted. The buzzing in his head, though fainter, didn't bother him as much as his leg. He had lost his way among the trees and was thirsty again. The pain in his leg and dryness of his throat and tongue were all he could think about. Tired and thoroughly wet he lay down close to a pine tree and fell asleep.

Zack had no sense of time now. At first he felt hot when he awoke and then cold as night fell. Once it rained, and Zack lay on his back and let the drops fall into his open mouth. Afterward he slept. He didn't like Minnesota. It was cold, and there were too many trees. As soon as he found Ben he would go back.

He no longer knew if it was night or day or how long he slept. The ground under him turned from ice to fire and to ice again. His throat burned while his body shook. "Don't worry," Chaplain Turner said from behind his desk, his dark face glistening. "Trust Jesus, you hear me, boy?"

As the chaplain's face disappeared another leaned over him, and a hand reached out to shake him. "You dead or alive?" Zack wanted to keep his eyes open, but he couldn't. Instead he groaned.

A tall thin girl dressed in a ragged cotton skirt and a man's coat too big for her bent over Zack. Her velvet skin was dark like his. Wonder shone in her large black eyes as Zack moaned. "You ain't dead yet, though you sure looks like it." Quick as a young deer the girl disappeared into the woods.

When she returned Zack was still lying where she had left him. An old woman, bent with age and her white face covered with wrinkles, hobbled behind the girl. Together they managed to lift Zack into an ancient handcart. His legs hung from its side. "Surely that boy is mighty sick. Don't know how that leg will do," the old woman said, looking at Zack's wounded leg. It was now swollen twice the size of the other. "Best get him on home so's I can get started." The girl nodded and began pushing the cart along the grassy path that only a sharp eye would have seen as a path.

A small cabin leaned close against an outcrop of rocks in a deep hollow protected by the mountains that surrounded it. A small barn stood nearby and behind that a rough wooden shack. Old hickory, ash, birch, and pines grew thick and close, hiding the fact that anyone lived there.

The cabin had a loft, a small bedroom with a rope bed, and one large room that served as kitchen and living room. A fireplace with an iron pot hanging in it took up most of one wall of the large room. Wooden stools, a rough-hewn table, and woven grass mats formed its simple furnishings.

Though Zack's body bore none of its former fat, even his bony weight proved a struggle for the two women, who laid him down on a mat close to the fire. Zack's ash-gray face and closed eyes gave no sign of life, but a faint moan now and then passed his lips. With gentle fingers the old woman examined the huge lump on the side of Zack's head. "Looks like this boy been struck in the head by somethin' or someone," she said. "It's a wonder he's still breathin'." Gently she eased Zack's head down and went to poke up the fire.

The girl sat next to Zack and watched him anxiously. "You reckon he's a runaway slave, Granny?" she whispered. "Ain't many coming through since Mr. Lincoln done set the slaves free."

"Might be he is, child. What Mr. Lincoln says don't make no mind to white folks in these hills who don't pay no call to northerners, including Mr. Lincoln. Some folks is ornery enough to shoot a colored man just 'cause they feel like it. Lost count of how many runaways going north we hid down here." Her white face wrinkled in a toothless smile.

"Mountain folks around here know I got two colored help living on my place, you and Lukus, but they never did know we were hiding slaves." The girl smiled. She had heard the stories of the old couple and their work for the underground railroad. It wasn't a real railroad but the name of a secret organization made up of folks who helped escaped slaves on their way north to freedom. Even after her old husband had died Granny kept on hiding slaves.

The old woman fingered Zack's army outfit. "Never seen a slave boy wearing Yankee blue pants. If he is a runaway might be he's running from the Yankee army. Just you come here and stir this pot so I can look at that boy's leg."

As the old woman unwound the clotted bootlaces and lifted the cloth from Zack's leg, he cried out. At the same time the sickening odor of decay made the girl's stomach heave. "It don't look good, child, it surely don't." The old woman shook her head at the sight before her. Thick yellow pus oozed from the wound where cracked, crusted black skin edged the gash.

For an hour the girl held the leg down while the old woman worked on it. Granny knew which mountain herbs and roots made good medicines, but this was the worst looking wound the girl had seen. Zack's cries and sobs filled the little shack with misery. He seemed not to see them when now and then his eyes flew open to look wildly about him.

Finally, the old woman stopped. "Ain't no more a body can do to clean out the poison. It's in the Lord's hands now, child." She reached for a clean cloth and folded it to make a compress for Zack's head. "Now we wait," she said. From under a pile of rags in a corner of the room she brought out a small corn-cob pipe and lit it by the fire with a piece of kindling stick. Seated with her back resting against the cabin wall she smoked her pipe. "Now where did that boy done come from?" she mused.

"Ain't nobody 'round here, 'cept you and me and Lukus, Granny. Nearest place is the widow's." Well hidden in the hills Granny's place was hard to find. It was hard to reach even for mountain folk who knew these thickly wooded hills and steep ravines. The girl shook her head. "Can't tell where he come from."

"Well, he ain't going nowhere, that's certain," the old woman said.

"How long you think Lukus be gone this time, Granny?"

"I 'spect when the good Lord brings him, child, he'll show up. Winter's coming on fast, and that's bad for folks what's going north through the mountains. Old Lukus be home directly, soon as he delivers them children and their mama along the line. Better go put up the chickens for the night, Marcy child."

Marcy got up, her thoughts on the mother and children Lukus was guiding to West Virginia. The woman hoped to find her husband and two sons who had escaped before President Lincoln's law that freed the slaves. It wasn't safe for colored strangers in these Virginia hills, even though the law said they were free. Lukus knew where to go. But if folks found out what Lukus did or that Granny and her man had worked for the underground railroad, they might come in the night and burn down Granny's barn, maybe even her cabin. Marcy shuddered. She pulled her coat tighter and went outside to tend the chickens.

16

In the Hollow

Winter came, and the first snows covered the little hollow that was now Zack's home. But where had he lived before the hollow? If only he could remember something from his past, anything. He tried to think and make himself remember, but it was as if a thick wall stood blocking all memories of his life before he had come to the hollow.

Wrapped in a sweater Granny had given him, Zack huddled close to the warmth of the cooking fire. The cold seeped through the thin walls of the cabin in spite of the mud and grasses stuffed between its cracks. The fire felt good on his leg. It was so thin now it looked like a stick to Zack. Carefully he rubbed the stiffness below the knee and then down the back of the leg. A thick poultice still covered the wound, though it no longer oozed and had begun to heal. His head, too, was better.

"I say you are doing mighty fine, son" the old woman crooned from the corner where she sat pounding nuts in a wooden bowl.

Zack looked up and nodded. "Yes'm, guess I am, thanks to you."

She chuckled deep in her throat, then said softly, "You just thank the Lord. It ain't what Granny done that kept you in this world. Didn't think you'd be with us long the way that fever took hold of you."

"Reckon so, Granny," Zack agreed. For weeks Granny and the girl called Marcy had nursed him in the little cabin while he lay half alive. When he had finally come around he had no idea where he was. Zack frowned. Once more he tried to remember, but it was like everything from the past had disappeared. He didn't even know if he had a name or where he had come from. Maybe he was a runaway. But how had he gotten into Union army pants and boots? There was nothing to identify him. Marcy said she had found him in the middle of nowhere and Granny had helped bring him to the cabin. He knew she had worked on his leg. Little by little his strength was returning, but his memory was a blank.

The door to the cabin opened, and Marcy came in carrying a sack over her thin, bony shoulder. "Granny, better be bringing in the goats tonight. It's powerful cold out there." She lowered her sack to the floor and dug out a handful of wrinkled, brown apples. "Hey, Blue, you ain't had nothing till you taste one of these roasted." She laid the apples in Zack's lap.

"Sounds right enough to me," he said. Because of his Union army clothes she had called him Blue from the first day he opened his eyes. It was as good a name as any. Skillfully, Zack laid the apples close to the heat of the fire to roast them. Somewhere, someplace he had learned to do that. He seemed to be good at tending the fire too, as if he had done it all his life. Now that he could hobble around and didn't fall asleep half the day, he tried to help the old woman and the girl with some of the heavy chores like loading the wood box.

Their meals were simple, usually beans and a kind of flat bread that tasted a little like fried corn cakes mixed with some kind of nuts and eggs. Dried roots, herbs, apples, and last year's corn and beans stored for winter in the root cellar below the cabin added to their meals. The thing Zack missed most was salt. There was none, and Zack knew it, but how he knew about salt was a mystery.

Sometimes Marcy brought up smoked fish or deer meat, even a bit of cured bacon now and then. "Lukus hires out in the spring to help with plantin'," she explained. "Sometimes he brings home a ham. Farmers 'round here like to pay in goods. Most times Lukus trades for what Granny and us be needin'. Granny's garden grows most things, and we be findin' lots of wild things growin' in these mountains that be good for a body."

Zack laughed at the way Marcy treated her chickens. When he helped her gather the eggs she hovered over the chickens like a mother hen. He shook his head when she praised them for the eggs they laid as if they had done her a special favor.

The goats, too, came under Marcy's motherly hand. One morning she showed Zack how to milk the nanny goat. The young goat eyed Zack as if she didn't trust him. Marcy's laugh sounded like a kind of music, merry and sweet. Zack liked to hear her laugh. Kneeling by the nanny goat he made faces and tickled the goat's neck under the chin.

"You gonna be here all day clownin' like that, and Granny waitin' for the milk?" Marcy scolded, but she laughed too. Zack kept on making her laugh until she pushed him aside and began the milking. The cheese Granny made from some of the milk had a powerful smell and a strong taste to Zack. He was used to it now, though at first he had not liked it.

After supper, Granny smoked her pipe and whittled with her knife, while Marcy worked on a brown dress she was sewing. Often Granny told them stories about the old days and her husband. "Used to be a fine strong man till the fever took him," Granny said. "Weren't nary a thing that man couldn't do. I remember when Lukus first came to us he was just a lad shaking for fear of us white folks. That boy had been on the run so long he didn't know how he got to us. My old man took him fishing in the creek at the crack of dawn. The two of them just set and fished for hours. That boy didn't want to leave after that." She chuckled. "Fact is, he never did go north. My man traveled clear to Snyder Crossing and dropped the word he got himself some colored help. Folks figured we bought ourselves a slave boy, and we didn't tell them different." Granny smoked her pipe in silence for a while as if she were remembering other times from the old days.

"That Lukus," she finally said, "he and my old man got on together like they was kin. Lukus is a real comfort to me with my man gone." As she spoke her fingers grew still and her eyes seemed to see something far in the past.

To Zack the warmth in the cabin and the quiet of the hollow made a little world sheltered from prying eyes. It felt safe here. No wonder the boy Lukus had not wanted to leave. "You always live in this hollow?" he asked.

Granny laughed and took the pipe from her mouth. "Times was hard when my old man and me was sprouts like you young uns. We was born and raised clear the other side of Snyder Crossing beyond Wickers Mountain. The winter of the big blizzard the sickness took my folks and kin. We wasn't married yet, not till the preacher came through in spring, but after that we lit out. Built this cabin in the hollow near a good stream. My man liked a place where a body could live and not be always bumping into his neighbor's land."

Marcy laughed lightly. "Sure don't be bumping into folks around here." She turned to Zack and studied his face. "Course, we did almost fall right over you lying out there in the woods. You came just like these goats and chickens Lukus brung home." She rubbed the soft skin of one of the young goats lying close to her feet. "On one of his trips north he'd stumbled on these goats and chickens just walkin' 'round loose in the woods. He watched for a whole day and night to see who might be comin' for them, but nobody came. Lukus knew for sure some wild animal gonna get them if he don't do somethin'. The way Granny put it, the good Lord watched over them poor things till Lukus came to rescue 'em."

Marcy laughed lightly, and Zack listened to her and smiled at her happiness. Sometimes the three of them laughed over Granny's stories till the tears ran down their faces. Though Zack had heard about Lukus, Granny had not yet told Marcy's story. The fire blazed prettily, and Zack felt its warmth where he sat trying to carve a bit of wood into a whistle. Marcy bit off a piece of thread and examined the hem she was sewing. Quietly Zack asked her, "Marcy, how'd you come to live here in the hollow?"

Marcy's face grew still and her eyes sad. "Seems like Lukus found me same as the chickens and the goats," she said.

"Now, girl, don't you be forgetting the Lord kept you safe so's Lukus could find you before some greedy bounty hunter come 'long. You was all wrapped in a woven mat just like the baby Jesus wrapped in the picture in the big Bible. Yes'm, your mama loved you and she knew you'd be all right," Granny comforted her.

Marcy's eyes filled with tears, and Zack wondered who would leave a little baby alone like that.

Granny rocked back and forth as she said, "Yes'm, your mama lay down next to you and went to sleep while the angels watched over you. When Lukus come, he knew she was gone to be with Jesus. Ain't nobody look like your mama did, lessen they see heaven open and the Lord Jesus waiting for them."

Marcy wiped her eyes with the back of her hand. "My mama's buried on one of them mountains near the West Virginia border. Someday, when there ain't no more war and it's safe to travel, Lukus is gonna show me where he marked her grave."

Zack swallowed hard. Had his mother died and left him alone in the woods? But why was he wearing a Union army outfit, and how had he come to hurt his leg? He turned his face away to stare at the fire. Why couldn't he remember?

That night while the others slept, he lay awake thinking about what Marcy had said. He lay close to one of the small goats, comforted by its warm body in spite of its strong smell. Would he end up like Marcy, living here without a past? Someone knocked gently on the cabin door, and Zack sat up cold with fear.

"That you, Lukus?" Granny called.

"It's me, old woman, and I'm plum froze to death." The door opened, and in the glow of the firelight Zack saw an old colored man with broad shoulders, a little stooped but still strong. "Ain't never knowed a winter like this one," he said. He stomped his feet and shut the door behind him.

In the excitement that followed, Marcy built up the fire, and Granny, dressed in her nightclothes and a warm robe, heated strong tea for the man called Lukus. He looked about done in with weariness.

After Lukus opened his sack and presented Granny with a bag of real flour and Marcy with a new bowl and cup, he turned to Zack. "Now, who be this young one?"

"Found him near dead with a leg wound, and nearly lost him to the fever," Granny said. "Looks like the good Lord sent him same way he sends whatever he has a mind to."

Lukus smiled a wide smile. "Expect that's good enough for me. You be right welcome, son." Lukus warmed his hands over the fire while he talked. Marcy handed him a plate of vittles and sat down by Zack. Lukus bowed his head and prayed aloud, thanking the Lord for all his gifts to his children.

In spite of the howling wind outside, Zack felt a warmth and goodness that seemed to come from the man. Marcy fixed a place near the fire for Lukus before she and Granny went back to their own beds. Zack drew his blanket over his head to keep in the warmth. Tomorrow he would ask Lukus if there was any news anywhere of a missing boy. Maybe Lukus could help him figure out what he ought to do.

The day came with a cold so sharp the firewood split with a single axe stroke. Zack kept moving while he helped Marcy with the daily chores. Most of the day they stayed inside the cabin.

Lukus rested and whittled on a box he was making. When Zack finally asked Lukus what he thought he ought to do, Lukus was silent for a moment before he answered.

"Looks to me, Blue, like you done have yourself a problem," he said. "If you a Union army boy, then by rights you got to get back to your unit. On the other hand, we don't know what that unit might be, or if somebody give you them clothes or something else." He paused to light his pipe. "Anyways, don't need to fret none till spring. A body can't do nothing but sit tight for now. This last trip 'most caught me off guard. Another hour out there last night, and you be finding me in them woods." Zack stared down at his ragged army trousers. Granny had sewed up the large gash where his leg had been hurt. Blood stains still showed darker than the cloth around them. A new thought made him anxious. What if somewhere there was a unit with his name listed? If only he knew his name!

17

Going Home

Spring came softly to the little hollow in the Virginia woods. Tender new green growth was everywhere. Zack welcomed the greens Granny cooked now, their first all winter.

Lukus was leaving to find work. "Got to shake Old Man Winter out of my bones. Might be gone a few days," he said as he left.

Granny, with her hands on her hips, called after him, "Can't wait for news of this here war, you mean. You be careful, old man." She turned back to the door. "'Spect the Lord got something for you to be doing," she mumbled. Zack was grinning, and Granny playfully swatted him. "Don't you stand here, boy, with all that work waitin' for two strong hands."

Two weeks later, Lukus burst into the small clearing just as Zack finished repairing a chicken roost. Granny hurried out of the shack into the warm sunshine. Marcy followed.

Lukus held up both of his hands and shouted, "The war be over anytime now! Praise the Lord!" Tears streamed down the old man's face. "General Lee done surrendered his army to General Grant."

134

Granny fell on her knees with cries of "Praise you, Lord."

Lukus hugged Marcy and pounded joyfully on Zack's shoulder. "At last we is really free, son," he said.

All of them were laughing and crying at the same time. Marcy spun about the clearing in a wild dance. Zack clapped crazily for her. The war was over.

Without any notice at all Zack suddenly remembered. Shawn's face flashed before his eyes, and the wagon train, and the raiders racing to attack it. He remembered the camp where he, Zack, shared a tent with Jeb the cook. "Zack! My name is Zack!" he cried out.

Lukus and Granny stood still. Marcy stared at him, but Zack couldn't stop his memories now. Did his friend Ben know he was missing? Maybe they all thought he was dead.

For half an hour Zack filled in his life story for Lukus and Granny and Marcy. "After Mosby's Rangers chased us I don't remember much until I woke up here," Zack finished.

Lukus puffed on his pipe before he spoke. "Looks like we needing to get you on to Washington so you can find out where you supposed to be, son."

Marcy's dark eyes widened. "But if the war be over, why can't he stay here with us?"

Granny took her own pipe from her mouth. "I reckon, child, if'n he wants to stay he is as welcome as spring."

"Won't do, old woman," Lukus said gently. "This boy wearing an army uniform, and till they lets him go by the law he be in the army." Lukus looked at Zack. "Ain't that so, son?"

In his heart the desire to stay in the hollow with Marcy and Lukus and Granny warred with what he knew was right. Zack nodded. "Reckon Lukus is right. I'm either listed as a dead man or a deserter." Both thoughts felt worrisome.

"We know as how you ain't a deserter, and looks like you ain't dead neither," Lukus said, then laughed. "Far as I can see we best get you to Washington so as the army can tell what you rightfully be." Zack laughed as Granny and Marcy, too, joined in the joke.

By morning Zack was ready to go. In his hand he held the stout walking stick Lukus had made for him and the food Granny had packed for them. Shyly he kissed Granny, who threw her arms about him.

"The Lord brung you to us, and the Lord is taking you where you have to go. You just trust him, child." She stood back from him and studied his face for a moment. "Might not see you this side of heaven, son, but Granny won't forget you."

Zack swallowed hard. "I won't forget you either. You and Marcy saved my life. If I can, I'll come back someday and visit you." He extended his hand to Marcy. Her hand in his was warm and strong. Words wouldn't come, and Zack looked at her helplessly.

Marcy smiled a slow smile that lifted the corners of her full mouth. "I wish you didn't have to go, Blue. Guess you have to. Maybe when you come back I'll still be here taking care of them pesky chickens."

Zack nodded and turned away unable to say more.

At the edge of the clearing he and Lukus stopped as Zack turned to wave one more time to Granny and Marcy. Granny looked small beside the tall thin form of Marcy, who raised her hand in a gentle wave. Behind them the morning mists lifted into a golden sun above the hollow. Zack would never forget that picture.

"Lukus," he said forcing himself away northward, "how long you reckon till we get to Washington?"

"'Most a week, but can't say for sure. One thing I be certain 'bout, 'fore we get there you be mighty sore carrying that pack 'cross your shoulder like that." He chuckled and pointed to his pack neatly slung across his back.

Zack shrugged his shoulder to test the rope. "Guess mine's not so heavy as yours. Feels okay to me."

"We'll see, we'll see," Lukus stated. He pointed with his walking stick toward the hills ahead of them. "This a mighty pretty world, but a body can get lost if he don't mind what he's doing out here. You pay 'tention now, son."

By late afternoon Zack had shifted his pack from shoulder to shoulder several times. It seemed to grow heavier with every mile.

As they walked Lukus showed Zack the secrets of the woods. Pointing to a large anthill he said, "Ants knows where to build.

They picks the warm side of the trees, the south." Passing poplar trees he slowed down to say, "See this kind of tree, how it be growing lightest on the one side, darkest on the other? Dark side be north, lightest be south." Zack was indeed learning.

"Most times," Lukus went on, "tops of them pine trees bending east." At the foot of a hill he stopped to point out the dense growth. "See there— that's a powerful lot of growin'. That be the south side of the hill. North side things growing taller and more openlike."

Zack had almost given up hope that they would stop short of dark, when Lukus took off his pack and laid it on the ground. "We best be camping here for the night," he said. "Tomorrow we be following a game trail right around the worst places. The Lord gave the good sense to animals so they knows the easiest way round. And he give me sense enough to follow them." He chuckled. "Now you and me going to make a good shelter for the night. Still gets cold nights 'round here." Lukus chose two young saplings that grew close enough to each other and connected the two with a long branch that he rested in a crook on each of their lower limbs. He secured other stripped branches against the first to form the skeleton of a wall. Together they gathered enough pine boughs to form the wall of the shelter by weaving them here and there through the poles. Lukus placed more pine boughs on the ground in front of the shelter to serve as their beds. A few feet further away he had Zack build a campfire so that when they slept they were protected in back by their shelter and in front by the fire. More and more Zack admired the old man's skills in the woods.

On the following day, halfway through the morning, Zack put down his pack and rubbed his sore shoulder. One thing was sure, Lukus knew what he was talking about.

As the days went by, Zack felt a new strength in his legs. He was beginning to enjoy being in the woods with Lukus. He had almost forgotten to think about what might be facing him in Washington. The shattering of the peace that had surrounded them came all too soon.

18

The Death of the President

An hour after the first light of dawn Lukus led the way to the bridge that crossed the Potomac River and into Washington, D.C. "Looks like somethin's goin' on," Lukus said, standing still. Though it was still early, a crowd was already forming, some on horseback, some in wagons, and most on foot. Lukus and Zack fell in step with a large group of black folks. All of them wore signs of mourning—narrow strips of black crepe tied around their upper arms.

"What is goin' on here?" Lukus asked.

"Mercy, mercy!" an old woman cried out, "Ain't you heard, man? They done shot President Lincoln!"

Lukus wept openly, and Zack felt his own tears streaming. How could it be? Who would kill the president, the man who had freed the slaves? A heavy weight sat on Zack's chest. A man beside the woman nodded his head sorrowfully. "It's true. The president is dead. We goin' now to watch the funeral train pass. They gonna take him home to Illinois where he come from." The man shared what details he knew of the grisly shooting of the president as he and his wife sat in Ford's Theater. Zack could hardly believe it.

"Come on, boy," Lukus said. With his hand gripping Zack's shoulder Lukus followed the others across the bridge.

In the distance Zack could see the white dome of the Capitol building towering over the city. On this side of the Capitol, rising above the swampy marshes close to the bank of the river, a half-built stone tower soared one hundred-fifty feet into the air. "That be the Washington Monument," the woman next to Zack informed him. "Never did finish it," she added.

From the plank bridge they stepped onto a dirt street turned to mud from the light rain falling. It was the widest street Zack had ever seen. Lukus was ahead of him, and Zack followed blindly through the crowds. When they turned onto Pennsylvania Avenue it seemed even wider to Zack, though here the crowds were so thick there was less room to move. They found themselves on the south side of the avenue where dingy buildings and shacks and sheds backed onto a canal. The small restaurants and offices were all closed and draped with black crepe. On the north side of the avenue, above the heads of the crowd, Zack saw several large hotels. Trees lined both sides of the street, and Zack wished he could have climbed one for a better sight of the city.

"There's the president's house, boy." The woman who had first spoken to them on the bridge pointed up the avenue to a large house with a portico and tall white colums in front. Zack caught a glimpse of the house and the iron rail fence enclosing it before the crowd closed off his view. "Over there," she said pointing west of the president's house, "in them two big houses the army and the navy has got their offices. You walk right down from the president's house and you can see the palaces where the government post office and the patent office be. Next on Fifteenth Street, the big building where the work is goin' on be the Treasury Department. Down southwest of the canal they calls that the Island. Lots of poor folks livin' down there. That's Greenleaft Point where the Potomac and the Eastern Branch River meet. You can see the United States Arsenal, and near that is the big red building they calls the Smithsonian Institute." Zack nodded.

The woman seemed to know all about Washington, D.C. "You be new to town," she said. "You just remember the Negro section is up there north on Tenth Street. There be a lot of rich folk livin' in big houses out in the countryside. Government workers, they's livin' mostly in the boardin' houses."

From the little Zack could see because of the crowds, the city was a mix of great government buildings, houses, and businesses, some of them shabby and small, others like the large hotels prosperous looking. The streets of Washington were a mass of people wearing black armbands. Every shop, every house bore its symbol of mourning. Nothing was open for business. Zack had no idea where they should go. The sight of people packed in every direction as far as the eye could see confused him.

"The railroad be right down by the foot of Capitol Hill, but ain't no way we gonna get near there," the woman said.

"I 'spect we better pay our respects further out along the train tracks," Lukus said grimly.

Zack wanted to try to push their way in, but he followed Lukus. There was no hope of getting close to the depot, and all along the tracks the way was lined with mourners, including a black army regiment. Zack remembered standing with the men of Company B the day President Lincoln had visited the camp in Virginia. He felt a sting of regret that he was not in full uniform standing at attention with these men.

Farther outside of town they found a place where they could squeeze near enough to see the tracks. Here the crowds were mostly black folks. For three hours they stood waiting. A light drizzle fell, dampening clothes and chilling the onlookers. Zack felt as if his heart was cold. The sound of the heavy tolling church bells coming from all over the capital city floated overhead. At his side Lukus whispered, "There she comes."

An engine heavily draped in black led the way. American flags hung from each side. Over the center of the cowcatcher stood a large picture of Abraham Lincoln, its corners draped in black. Slowly the train moved by. Behind the engine each of the passenger cars was also draped in black. The car next to last held the coffin of the president. As it came in sight a man close to Zack stood to attention and saluted. Others did the same. Someone said in a choked voice, "Father Abraham be going home now." Zack was aware of the sounds of weeping all around him as his own tears fell. He thought of Abraham Lincoln's eyes as they had looked into his that day long ago.

Lukus said softly, "It be the end of a long journey." He looked down at Zack for a moment. "God's servant going home, son, and thanks to him we are free." Lukus turned to the train and saluted. Zack did the same. Not a man or woman moved till the train had made its lonely way out of sight.

On the way back to the city, Lukus and Zack learned the details of the president's death. Only five days after the surrender of General Robert E. Lee and his army to Union forces, President Lincoln had been shot by an actor who was bitter over the defeat of the South. Lukus shook his head sadly. "Can't think what sort of man kill the president of the United States. It was an evil day that man be born."

Zack was about to agree when a familiar voice hailed him. "That you, Zack?" The voice belonged to a young black soldier named Will, who stared in amazement at Zack.

"Will?" Zack couldn't believe his eyes. It was Will. As the man walked toward them Zack saw that he limped.

"I thought I was seein' a ghost." In his excitement the young soldier gripped Zack's shoulder as if to prove to himself that Zack was no ghost. "Never expected to see you, and here you turn up on this day of all days. Where you been, boy? Chaplain Turner got word from a friend of yours in Harpers Ferry, somebody by the name of Shawn, that you were dead. The chaplain told us you were killed by a raider while you were drivin' a wagon in them Blue Ridge Mountains. Only thing left to identify you was your army cap. How long you been here? And how'd you get here?"

"Came in with Lukus this morning. If we can all get out of this crowd I can explain." Will seemed to know the city and led them away toward the Negro section of town. As they walked Zack told his story.

"So," Zack said as he finished, "I guess I better be going along and turn myself in."

"Ain't no use you goin' anywhere today," Will said. "You and Lukus can stay with my folks till things open up around here again. Everything is closed 'count of the president's death. Took a bullet in the chest and one through my leg and got sent home. My folks' place is just across the way. You both be mighty welcome to stay as long as you like."

Zack waited anxiously for Lukus to say something. The old man looked tired. "I was thinkin' on headin' back, but I'm thinkin' now we would be right glad to stay at your place." Zack felt a great relief as he followed Will to a small shanty in the Negro section. "My folks will be down at the church helpin'. Ever since the president's death a lot of our people have been comin' into the city to pay their

respects. All the churches are helpin' to feed folks."
Will spread a cold supper for the three of them
which they ate in the cool of the tiny back yard.
Will's folks returned late, and the five of them talked
until the stars had come out and Zack could barely
keep his eyes open.

In the morning before the others were up Lukus
gently woke Zack. He placed a hand on Zack's shoulder. "Think I'd best be gettin' back. Things are goin' to
be all right, son. The Lord had his hand on you all this
time, and he ain't letting go of you now."

Zack nodded as his throat tightened. He managed
to whisper, "I won't forget you, Lukus, or Granny
or Marcy."

Lukus nodded. Without a further word he left. His
broad shoulders were straight, and his old pack was
slung carefully across his back. Zack felt a deep sadness as he watched him go.

At breakfast an excited Will appeared. "Fell asleep
last night thinkin' I forgot to tell you about Chaplain Turner." Zack looked up sharply. Had something happened to the chaplain?

"Reverend Turner is right here in Washington. Not
long after we heard the news about you, the chaplain
took a minié ball in the chest. A lot of us in Company
B were wounded that day at Petersburg. Chaplain
Turner recovered, but the army sent him back to
Washington and transferred him to a new job getting
volunteers to join the army. I hear he is one of the best
recruiters the army has got. I reckon we can find him
today over at the recruitment office."

Zack could barely believe his luck. Maybe there was still hope for him to work for Chaplain Turner. It wasn't until they reached the recruitment office that Zack began to worry. He had no proof of his story. What if the army decided he was a deserter?

Visions of jail and worse, floated in his head as he sat rigid on a chair in the outer office. An hour had passed since Will left him here. Chaplain Turner was in a meeting, and Zack had explained his case to the man in charge. At the sound of a footstep his heart leapt into his throat.

Chaplain Turner! "Well, son, the Lord was watching over you, and he has brought you back. I'm mighty glad to see you. Now the question is what to do with you. I'm afraid I am no longer in a position to use you. Officially you are listed as dead, and here you are alive and well. The problem is, in spite of the difference between you and your grandmother on your correct age, you are too young to be in this army under the present laws. I fear the best I can do for you, son, is see to it that you are mustered out of the army with the pay that is due you."

Zack didn't know what to think. He swallowed hard and nodded. "Yes, sir."

"These are sad times for our people, for our country, son. Without President Lincoln at the head of our nation we face an uncertain future. He was a friend to our people." The chaplain paused. "My advice to you is to go home, learn all you can, and be a credit to our people. I recall you and Reverend Stewart Able's family were good friends. I received a letter from the reverend after notifying him of your supposed death. He had high hopes for you, son."

Zack thought of Ben and his father. Maybe he could go to Minnesota, at least for a visit.

Chaplain Turner smiled as if he had read Zack's thoughts. "I shall telegraph Reverend Able the good news of your return this afternoon. I am certain Reverend Able will be eager to see you. Let me see what arrangements we can make. Your army pay will be more than enough to cover your travel expenses. That reminds me of something I was intending to do. Come along inside the office."

From a closet inside his office the chaplain brought out a large box. After a moment's search he held up an army cap and jacket. "These are yours, son. The army sent them to me after the wagon was taken back from the raiders. I planned to send them on to your friend Ben for keepsakes, but here you are to take them yourself." He handed the cap and jacket to Zack.

Zack brushed his hand over the rough blue cloth. The numbers on the jacket and cap were his. "Never thought I would see these again," he said.

Chaplain Turner cleared his throat. "Well, I believe I can pull some strings here in Washington to see that you get what pay is due you. Where are staying, son?"

Zack gave the chaplain his friend's name. The thought of being paid by the army what was owed him hadn't entered Zack's mind. "It feels kind of funny," he said. "Me being in the army one minute and out the next. I guess, I'll miss it some. Leastwise, you and Caleb and the others."

Reverend Turner looked suddenly older than he had. His eyes grew sad. "Caleb was a fine boy. He died bravely."

Zack gasped and tears came to his eyes. "Will didn't tell me."

"I expect he didn't want to burden you all at once." The reverend's voice grew softer. "We lost over half of Company B at Petersburg."

Zack could feel himself trembling, and his voice was no more than a whisper as he asked, "Moses?"

"Yes, son, Moses was one of the first to fall, a brave leader." Chaplain Turner's eyes, too, overflowed with tears. He patted Zack's shoulder. "It is all right to cry, son."

After a while Zack wiped his eyes and face with his hands.

Chaplain Turner handed him a handkerchief. "Freedom has come with a terrible price, son. We must never forget."

As Zack walked back to Will's place, his heart felt heavy. Some part of him would never be the same again. He would never forget.

19

An End and a Beginning

Some of the people who had come to Washington, D.C., for the president's funeral had left, but everywhere Zack looked he saw crowds of Union soldiers. Will explained as they walked to the train depot. "A lot of them are goin' home now that their army time is over. Some of them are comin' out of the hospitals and headin' back to their units. You can almost tell by their faces the ones goin' home."

Zack felt for his army discharge papers and pushed them deeper into his pocket along with the telegraph Ben's father had sent in answer to Reverend Turner's. The telegraph read, "Praise the Almighty. Come home, Zack. Will meet you in St. Paul." The chaplain had seen to the arrangements for Zack's travels. Inside Zack's shirt his army pay and train tickets were safe in a pouch. He would still have to purchase a ticket in Illinois for the Mississippi River steamboat to St. Paul.

"You sure you got everythin'?" Will inquired anxiously.

Zack shifted the large box Will's folks had packed with biscuits, cold meat, cheese, boiled candy, a whole pie, boiled eggs, and sausage enough to last him half the trip. His canteen was filled with fresh water. They had also stuffed him well before he left with eggs and bacon, grits, and biscuits with honey and fresh milk. "Thanks to your folks I'm well supplied," Zack said heartily.

"Now you know, you got to keep your money out of sight. These be hard times for a lot of folks," Will cautioned. Zack nodded and patted his shirt. A thief would have to go right through him before he could get to the money. He eyed the men pouring into the train station, some of them black, most of them white, and not a few of them already full of whiskey. It wasn't poor folks he worried about, but drunken soldiers like Sergeant Dole could be trouble.

From a train window Zack waved a last time at his friend Will, then settled back onto the seat. He was on his own now. The train was crowded, and the coach Zack chose was filled with Negro soldiers. Zack shared his seat with a thin, weary-faced black man whose leg stuck out awkwardly stiff and straight before him. "Wounded at Fort Fischer, North Carolina," he informed Zack.

Across from them a young Negro, dark-skinned and carrying a crutch, pulled up his pant leg to expose a deep ugly wound that had taken off part of the man's calf. "Got this near Richmond," he said. Within minutes the two soldiers were swapping stories. As Zack listened he remembered what it was like after the battle of New Market when the newly wounded came back from battle. He thought of Captain Hale, and a sadness came over him.

In the aisle and all around, men joined in telling their tales of the war. Zack had little need to do more than listen. Over and over he heard someone say, "I have seen the elephant." It meant they had been in the heavy fighting. He hoped no one would ask him about his time in the army. Who would want to hear about a chaplain's assistant or a mule team driver? Of course, he might have mentioned Jeff's rescue or the Mosby raiders, but what was that compared to a real battle and being shot?

Mostly everyone slept the best they could in the overcrowded coaches. After hard army bunks and the packed earth of tent floors, Zack fell asleep easily slumped against the wooden train seats. At mealtimes the train stopped for food at places called railroad houses, small hotel restaurants. Zack's box of food was soon gone, and he discovered that the brief stops were usually at places serving food much like army fare at its worst. The leaden biscuits, known as sinkers, like the army bread called hardtack, had to be soaked so a person could eat them.

"Wish these here railroad people would put their heads together and come out with a train that don't end every few miles," the young man sitting across from Zack remarked. Zack smiled. It was true that at the end of one railroad company's line passengers were discharged onto the next company's line to continue their journey. Sometimes the wait for the next train was an hour or two, and sometimes a whole day. Zack used the time to stretch his legs and walk about. It did not occur to him that anything might go wrong.

It was the end of the line, and the train was pulling into a town not much different looking than most of the towns they had passed. The train belonging to the next railroad company wasn't due in for another two hours. The depot stood close to the rest of the town. It was near noon, and a lot of the passengers who had been on the last train with Zack were heading into town for a meal. Zack needed to use the depot's outhouse first. As he left the outhouse, two white men, who looked like they might be farmers or workers, stared at him. Zack knew better than to stare back.

The depot was deserted, and with lowered eyes he turned toward the main street of town and walked quickly toward the small hotel restaurant. The sound of footsteps behind him made him glance back. The two white men were following him. At least they were coming his way. The restaurant was crowded, but Zack managed to find a seat with three other black soldiers he had seen on the train. From the corner of his eye he saw the two white men sitting near the door.

The meal was great. Hot stew with biscuits, preserves, strawberry pie, and a pitcher of fresh milk thick with cream. Zack sat as long as he could. His companions had already left.

Glancing up Zack saw that the two white men were still seated by the door and were looking his way. He ought to have left with his companions. Without looking down at his shirt Zack managed to slip out his money. He counted out what he needed and quickly slid the rest back inside his shirt. He tried not to look around as he paid his bill. With relief he noted that the men no longer sat at the door. Maybe they hadn't been interested in him at all, just hungry. Anyway, he would soon be safely back at the station. With a shock he saw that the two men were lounging against the outside wall of the hotel and looking his way.

Zack went quickly around the opposite corner of the hotel and hurried into the outhouse in back. His fingers fumbled as he undid his money pouch and stuffed the money and remaining train ticket into his boots. From the dirt floor of the outhouse he scooped several small stones and pebbles. He stuffed them into the pouch along with some folded bits of torn newspaper someone had left in the outhouse. He replaced the pouch inside his shirt and breathed a quick prayer.

The two men were waiting outside the outhouse. No one else was in sight. "Not so fast," one of them said as Zack tried to run. The man grabbed him by the shirt and tore it open exposing Zack's money pouch. His voice was low and menacing. "Now, where do you suppose this young thief got all that money we saw him with inside the hotel restaurant?" He laughed unpleasantly. "I'll just be taking it for safekeeping," he said shoving the pouch deep into his pocket. His hand still gripped Zack's shirt tightly about Zack's neck. "If you know what's good for you, just get on out of here. This town don't hold with coloreds that steal. You say anything to anyone and likely I'll see you swinging from a tree before nightfall." Zack tried to nod. "This is our town, you understand?" Again Zack nodded.

"Get going," the other man said, "before we change our minds and feed you to the hounds." With a rough shove the soldier released Zack. In a flash Zack was off running to the depot.

Any minute the two men might discover Zack's pouch full of stones and paper. He had to hide quickly. His body trembled as he wove his way through the gathering passengers to a group of Negro soldiers waiting for the train. Most of them were men from the last train, and Zack knew a few of them. A whistle screeched loudly in the distance. The train was rolling into the station! Keeping as close as he could to the Negro soldiers, he managed to get aboard. He still had his ticket and his money. He knew the two white men might still try to follow him, and all he could do was hope they would not dare. This time he refused a window seat. Several times Zack feared that any moment the two white men would come and drag him from the train. Would his companions fight for him? He looked hopefully at the young man with the heavy crutch who had seen his share of fighting. With a lurch the train moved and the whistle blew. They were on the way out of the station at last. Zack leaned back and for the first time in the last two hours he let his body go limp. Sometime during the next hour he remembered a little debt he had not payed, more like a big debt. "Thank you, Lord," he whispered. "I know you was watchin' over me back there."

Outside, the land rolled by mile after mile. Zack's thoughts slipped back to the hollow and Marcy. He pictured her standing next to Granny, her hand lifted to wave good-bye. His mind shifted to Ben, and he wondered how many more miles it would be to St. Paul.

Zack stretched his cramped legs. He knew he had grown some, maybe an inch or so. Most likely Ben was taller too. They hadn't seen each other for over a year. Had Ben changed? Ben's family had always treated him like kin, but what would the people of Bellfield be like? He supposed white folks there treated blacks the same ways white folks in New York City or in the army did. There were good and bad people in both places. He looked down at the dark, calloused skin of his hands. He had learned a lot in the army. He thought of Chaplain Turner, of Moses, and of old Lukus, all good men. It didn't matter what color his skin was.

In Rock Island, Illinois, he left the train and walked to the river to buy his steamboat ticket. At the landing a large white steamboat with the name *Princess* across its two giant paddlewheels was already filling with passengers, most of them soldiers returning north. Zack had been on a steamboat once with Ben, but this one was larger. The main deck had huge paddlewheels, and Zack could see giant stacks of freight stored in back of the deck's boilers and machinery. The passenger deck above it had a veranda that ran along the outside of the passenger cabins. On the third deck, called the hurricane deck, were cabins for the boat's officers, and ahead of them two giant black smokestacks. On top of the officers' cabins was the pilot house crowning all. A loud warning whistle blew, and Zack hurried to buy his ticket. "You got your money, boy?" the ticket agent demanded.

"Yes, sir," Zack said quickly. He held up his money for the man to see.

"That will be enough for deck passage back of the freight, same deck as the boilers and engines," the man said. Zack thanked him, took his ticket, and hurried to the gangplank. The quarters for the deck passengers, though cheaper, were bare cupboards with straw mats. Zack made his way past the boat's kitchens to where several black workers lounged. They were the men known as roustabouts, who loaded and unloaded freight. Zack was welcomed as soon as the men saw his Union army uniform. In the lazy hours between stops for wood or passengers the men swapped stories. By the end of the trip Zack had joined his new friends and slept in the open air of the deck. He shared their simple food cooked over a small stove and sometimes helped with the loading of firewood at stops along the river.

When the big boat finally glided into place along the St. Paul docks, Zack spotted a familiar figure among the waiting folks. It was Ben's father! A lump settled in Zack's throat. Ben wasn't with his father.

Pastor Able met him at the foot of the gangplank. Before Zack could speak, Ben's father's arms were tight around him in a great bear hug. "We never thought to see you on this earth again, son," he said in a husky voice. "Now, I want to hear all about everything as soon as you have had a good meal. We've a ways to go to Bellfield, and our first stop better be for some food."

"Right," Zack agreed. Ben's father's long strides took them quickly down the street to a small hotel restaurant. Inside they sat at a small table. While they ate, Zack talked, and Ben's father listened.

Back in Bellfield shadows filled the barn where Ben sat waiting, listening to the sounds of the wind moving a loose board and the scurrying of mice in the hay. He sat motionless, almost invisible in the semidarkness. His thick brown hair and brown shirt blended into the wood stall where he sat. Across his knees lay the army knife Zack had sent him a year ago. The rag he was using to polish it had fallen to the floor unnoticed. Ben ran his hand over the smooth wooden handle, then slid the blade into its leather sheath attached to his belt. He wanted Zack to see he still had it. The memory of the day the news had come informing them that Zack was presumed dead passed before his mind.

The wooden cross Ben had built and placed in a corner of the cornfield as a marker for Zack was still out there. The telegraph that Zack was alive had left Ben openmouthed, unable to believe it at first. For days afterward he thought and dreamed of how it would be when Zack came back.

He ought to be out looking for a sight of the wagon right now. Instead, he continued to sit in the barn where he had been for the past two hours. Zack's bed was set up in the loft next to Ben's. Twice Ben had checked his fishing poles, one for Zack and one for himself. As soon as Zack was settled in tomorrow they could take off. He would show him the new raft his friend Jamie and he were making. Everything was ready, at least he hoped it was. The two of them had always done things together until Zack went off to the army.

Ben leaned back against the barn wall. The big question was, Would Zack want to stay in Minnesota now that he had been in the army? The sound of a shout brought him to his feet. It was his father's voice. They were here!

The wagon pulled up in the front yard. His mother was running toward it. Ben swallowed hard and then he was running too.

As the wagon lurched to a stop Zack's heart pounded. Had Ben changed? He had been gone for over a year, and maybe things were different now with Ben. He swallowed hard. Part of him wanted to jump down and run toward his friend shouting for joy. The other part wanted to pretend it didn't matter if Ben wouldn't want that anymore. His throat felt dry and his legs weak. And then he saw Ben.

As Zack stepped from the wagon toward him, Ben came running. He threw his arms around Zack's shoulders and hugged him tight in a great bear hug. When Ben let go Zack was grinning his old grin.

Ben pummeled Zack's shoulder. "You are supposed to be lying out back in the cornfield. Least your tombstone is, and here you are big as life. Welcome home, Zack."

Ben's mother spoke through her tears. "We are so glad to have you here, our dear Zack. And to think you traveled all that way on your own!"

"I guess I did, didn't I?" Zack said. His voice grew husky, "Ain't no place I'd rather be than here." The struggle inside Zack fell away, and his eyes glistened with tears. "Reckon I missed you a powerful lot, Ben." He swallowed, then smiled. "You suppose we could take us a look at that cornfield? Ain't every fellow who gets to come home and see his own tombstone."